Lizzie shook her head. "I thought you understood, but you knew nothing about my life then, just as you know nothing about it now."

"As you know nothing about mine," Chico fired back, and as the temperature soared between them, she whirled around. She started to say something—something angry to hit back at him, something passionate to express all the hurt she'd felt when she was only fifteen—but as she speared a glance into Chico's blazing eyes, he reached out and caught her close.

She held her breath and stared up at him. He wouldn't dare— Surely, he wouldn't dare—

His grip tightened, and slowly and deliberately he brought her inch by reluctant inch to within a whisper of his mouth. And when he brushed her lips with his, she shivered and sighed, because she could do nothing else. It was a signal for him to move closer until his hard body could control hers, and resting his forearm on the wall above her head, he dipped his head to tease her with almost-kisses until she was helpless with desire. Need collected inside her until, finally, it overwhelmed her.

Welcome to the hot, sultry and successful world of Brazilian polo!

Get ready to spend many

Hot Brazilian Nights

with Brazil's sexiest polo champions!

Award-winning author Susan Stephens revisits the power of the international polo circuit in the land of samba, carnival and hot Latin lovers: *Brazil*! Forget privilege and prestige; this is Gaucho Polo—hard, hot and unforgiving, like the men who play the game!

These temptingly irresistible alphas work hard and play hard as they lead their team, the Thunderbolts, to victory. Off the field they're notorious heartbreakers, but what happens when they meet the one person who can tame that unbridled passion?

Find out in this sexy new series!

You may have already met gorgeous team captain Gabe in *Christmas Nights with the Polo Player*. Now get ready to meet the rest of the Thunderbolts—Chico, Tiago, Lucas and Karina—as they tackle tempers on the playing field and passions in the bedroom!

In the Brazilian's Debt
Available in March 2015

At the Brazilian's Command
Available in April 2015

Look out for Lucas and Karina's stories later in 2015!

Available from **Harlequin.com**

Or visit the author's website at
susanstephens.com/thunderbolt

In the
Brazilian's Debt

———

Susan Stephens

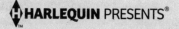

ISBN-13: 978-0-373-13324-6

In the Brazilian's Debt

First North American Publication 2015

Copyright © 2015 by Susan Stephens

Recycling programs for this product may not exist in your area.

Printed in U.S.A.

Susan Stephens was a professional singer before meeting her husband on the Mediterranean island of Malta. In true Harlequin Presents style they met on Monday, became engaged on Friday and married three months later.

Susan enjoys entertaining, travel and going to the theater. To relax she reads, cooks and plays the piano, and when she's had enough of relaxing she throws herself off mountains on skis, or gallops through the countryside singing loudly.

For my wonderful readers who love their bad boys safely confined within the covers of a book, Chico is for you.

CHAPTER ONE

REVENGE IS A dish best served cold.

Lizzie thought about her father's words as the transport plane lost height, bringing them closer to their destination. Determination was an admirable quality, her father had insisted with his usual bluff confidence, founded on nothing more than one of his hunches and the dregs from a bottle of Scotch. His Lizzie wasn't short of determination. She would rebuild the family pride where he had failed.

How many other apparently confident people put on an act in order to reassure others? Lizzie wondered as she peered out of the small, grainy window. She had been planning to embark on this advanced training programme with horses in Brazil for years, and just hoped she wasn't shooting too high. She *was* determined to set the family business back on its feet, but flying for hours over miles of uninhabited nothingness in Brazil had thrown her. She felt so far away from home, and seeing Chico Fernandez again after all these years was going to dent her confidence even more.

'How come you're not nervous?' Lizzie's friend and fellow groom Danny Cameron demanded, clutching on tightly to Lizzie's hand as the plane dropped like a stone.

She put on one hell of an act? She wasn't a great traveller, and probably felt the same fear as Danny. As the ground came up to meet them like a slap in the face, her stomach roiled. The distinctly unglamorous transporter, known as the Carrier Pigeon to the staff of Fazenda Fernandez, appeared to dive-bomb its target, which was a rambling ranch in the middle of the pampas in Brazil.

'We'll be fine,' she soothed Danny, hoping for the best. *Would they make it?*

Would she make it, more to the point? Never mind that the runway was short, and the plane was loaded down with horses, grooms, and equipment, all heading to the world-class training ranch of the infamous hard man of polo, Chico Fernandez. She might make it to the ground safely, but would she make it safely out of here with both her heart and her reputation intact? It seemed incredible now that Chico had once meant so much to her, but she'd been fifteen the last time she'd seen him in person, when, for one glorious summer, Chico had been her closest friend and confidant, until her parents started referring to him in the same tone people reserved for the devil.

Chico Fernandez was supposedly the Fane family's nemesis, yet here she was, to suck him dry of all his equine knowledge, according to her father, before returning home to restore the horse-training business that, again, according to her father, Chico Fernandez had destroyed. She knew now her father's bluster covered for his faults, and had learned to make up her own mind where his many, dramatic pronouncements were concerned. The college that had awarded her this scholarship to train with Chico Fernandez was spending good money on the course, as were all the other students. She guessed they, like her, also hoped to 'suck the famous polo player dry' of everything Chico could teach them.

Any thoughts her father might have had about this being a wonderful opportunity for Lizzie to get back at a man he considered his enemy were so far off the mark as to be ludicrous. But she'd listened patiently, as she always did when her father was on one of his rambles, as he assured her that this trip was simple justice, because Chico had stolen everything from him: his good name, his business, his wealth and success, and his horses. 'Chico took everything from me—*everything*, Lizzie—even your mother! Never forget that.'

How could she forget her father's impassioned speech, when he constantly reminded her that thanks to Chico he had been reduced to a drunken husk, while her mother had left him to go and live in the South of France with the latest in a long line of much younger men?

But not before her mother had been seduced by Chico? The rumours put about by her parents were even worse. They said Chico had forced her mother to have sex with him. Lizzie couldn't equate that with the man she'd known, though her mother, whom Lizzie had been made to call Serena, had done everything she could to destroy Lizzie's friendship with Chico, saying he was just a poor boy from the slums of Brazil, while her daughter was Lady Elizabeth Fane.

Lizzie had thought herself in love with Chico, and had cared nothing for her so-called status. She still cared nothing for it, but she was no longer a gullible adolescent and could see her parents' faults. Whatever her father said, Lizzie doubted Chico was to blame for her family's descent into ruin. In fact, her grandmother, who had taken over Lizzie's care when her parents lost interest, had confirmed this, saying Lizzie's parents hadn't needed any help where ruining the family was concerned.

What had hurt Lizzie the most was that Chico had promised to take her away from a home life that had frightened her, before her grandmother had moved back in, mainly because her parents had held parties where everyone got drunk and did things behind locked doors that Lizzie could only guess. She hadn't shared these suspicions with Chico, just her unease, though she had told him how much she hated living at home. As a youth looking for a cause, Chico hadn't demanded too much of an explanation, but had promised to rescue her, only to return to Brazil without even saying goodbye.

It was hard to reconcile the friendship they'd shared with the way she felt about him now. She had trusted Chico completely and had never got over what she'd seen as his betrayal. They had shared so many adventures on horseback, and had got to the point of exchanging silly gifts, though Chico's mentor, the Brazilian polo player, Eduardo Delgardo, had made sure their friendship never went any further than that.

The only way to deal with her mixed feelings for Chico, Lizzie decided, was to concentrate on the one thing that mattered, which was his magical way with horses. This gift had made him her hero when she was fifteen years old, and if she could pick up everything Chico could teach her here on his world-famous training course it could be the key to rebuilding the family business. She was looking forward to showing him how much she'd changed, from an impressionable teenager into an individual who was every bit as driven and as determined as he was, and, though it would be tough seeing him every day, failure wasn't an option when the people of Rottingdean were depending on her to get this right.

Her thoughts were interrupted when Danny yelped as the plane landed.

There was no going back now.

As she looked outside her confidence took another

knock. Everything was so much bigger and wilder than she had imagined, and potentially more dangerous.

Like Chico?

The ground was parched. The sun was blazing down. According to the weather forecast, the humidity outside the aircraft would be high. The horses would be restless after such a long confinement. They would need firm and sensitive handling by their grooms, which was where Lizzie excelled. Horses were her life, and seemed to sense how deeply she cared for them. Her presence alone was usually enough to reassure them. Unbuckling her seat belt, she was out of her seat before the pilot had turned off the engines.

Lizzie remained with the most fractious horse until the back of the plane had been opened and sunlight streamed in as the ramp was lowered into place—and the sound of a husky male voice, so familiar, so long in the past, issuing terse commands in Portuguese, froze her to the spot.

'Quem é que na parte de trás congeladas em pedra? Tremos trabalho a fazer!'

It stunned her to hear that voice again, though it had gained an edge of command. Chico was used to instant compliance, she gathered. He must expect it. He was so successful. For Lizzie it was a nostalgic reminder of the past, and for a moment she thought herself back at Rottingdean in the shade and the quietness of the stables, a fifteen-year-old girl, hanging on every word he said—

'Lizzie!'

Danny was shaking her arm, Lizzie realised, because, thanks to thinking about Chico, she had become the one fixed point in what was now a hive of activity. 'What did he say?'

Danny had a better command of Portuguese than she did, and lost no time translating for her. '"Who's that at the back of the plane, frozen into stone? We have work to do!"' 'Lizzie!' Danny muttered urgently. 'That's you!'

'Oh—' Red-cheeked, Lizzie stared around, but there was no sign of Chico.

He never had been the type to hang around, she remembered as she caught a glimpse of a big male figure, dressed in dark, form-fitting clothes, ducking into a high-powered Jeep. He was so much bigger than she remembered, and his body language had changed. Instead of the easy stride she remembered, everything about him was commanding and certain…

Well, he would be changed. Twelve long years had passed since the last time she'd seen Chico, though even as he drove away at speed now that brief glimpse of him was enough to make her heart race. Which was not the best of starts, if she was going to complete this course successfully. And she was not going home without a result. She would not be taken in a second time by Chico's seductive charm. She would focus on the horses, and make a strong business plan before returning to Scotland to make a name for herself.

Staring up into the solemn brown eyes of the horse she was caring for, she was relieved to see his ears pricked with interest, rather than laid back with fright. If only she could soothe herself the same way.

'Come on, handsome,' she coaxed. 'It's time for you and me to test the air of Brazil.'

He was content. He was back on his vast *fazenda* in Brazil, which was the most cherished part of his worldwide equine empire. Control and order ruled throughout. His control. His rule. Horses loved order and certainty, and he loved horses, so the smooth running of this ranch was non-negotiable.

'New recruits, Maria,' he snapped out crisply.

Crossing the wooden floor of his pristine office, his elderly secretary handed him a sheet of paper listing the new students.

He exchanged warm glances with Maria, who was the only woman in the world he trusted. Maria had been with him from the start. They adored each other. It was more a mother and son relationship than that of employer, employee. Maria had occupied a neighbouring shed in the *barrio*, the violent slum where they had both started out, where someone was murdered on average every twenty minutes. Maria's son, Felipe, and Chico's brother, Augusto, had been in the same gang, and had been shot dead in front of Chico in the same brutal incident. Chico had been ten years old at the time with a father in prison and a mother on the game. He had vowed to look after Maria, as he had vowed to bring justice and education to the *barrio*. He'd done both.

'So,' he mused, scouring the list. 'These brave few have come to study at Fazenda Fernandez so they can leave with a diploma stating they have survived and thrived beneath the riding boot of the acknowledged master of the equine world?' He exchanged an amused glance with Maria. 'And still they come, Maria.'

'Thanks to you, Chico,' Maria insisted. 'Because you are the best.' Maria's characterful mouth pressed down as she shrugged expansively. 'The best want to study with the best.'

He laughed. 'So, who have we got here?' His gaze stalled on one name. Thank God Maria hadn't noticed his reaction. Explanations would have spoiled her day. Seeing the name Fane and that distinctive address had spoiled his day. He had thought he was done with that family.

'There were more applicants than ever this year, Chico.'

He didn't want to upset Maria when she was in full flow. Maria was proud of him. She treated him like the son she had lost, and in return he loved Maria and protected her in every way he could. He would not upset her now, so a short hum was his only response to her rapid-fire résumé of each of the new students.

'And this one's from the *barrio*, Chico—'

'Good,' he murmured, still debating what to do with one particular student on the list. As for the *barrio,* that was an ongoing project and very close to his heart. It was a battle he'd never win, some said, but he refused to accept that. To be the best he could be was his personal goal; to help young people from all backgrounds was his mission in life.

'And we have a member of the British aristocracy with us this year—'

This he already knew. And he was a whole lot less impressed about that fact than Maria.

'No wonder,' Maria enthused. She was brandishing an official-looking document at him. 'Fazenda Fernandez is up for yet another award this year. We are even famous in Scotland where this aristocratic young lady comes from.'

'Really? That's good, Maria.'

He made a point of standing next to Maria as he read the letter over her shoulder to assure her of his interest. The letter confirmed that Lizzie Fane was a member of that year's new student intake. He smiled at first, remembering how Lizzie had teased him about his broken English, and how she'd patiently taught him, and how he'd loved those lessons. He had loved watching her mouth form the words more than the words themselves. It was a surprise he'd learned anything new, but Lizzie had assured him that he was her best student.

Her only student, he thought now, his hackles rising when he thought back to her parents, who hadn't liked

Lizzie to have any friends—in case they talked about what they saw at Rottingdean House, he had presumed at the time. They couldn't get rid of him, because he was with Eduardo, but they had targeted Chico, levelling the most terrible accusations against him in the hope of getting Eduardo to buy them off.

At the time he was angry with Eduardo and Lizzie's grandmother for spiriting him away before he'd had chance to clear his name, but now he realised they had saved him from going head to head with the establishment, which, back then, was a battle he could never have won. The only thing he didn't understand about that time was why Lizzie hadn't stepped forward to defend him. He had thought they were friends, but blood was thicker than water, it turned out, and she had chosen her lying, cheating family over him.

And now Lizzie was here on his ranch, hoping to benefit from his teaching? It was so incredible it was almost funny, but he wasn't in the mood for laughing.

'My success is thanks to you, Maria, and to the wonderful staff you have gathered around you,' he said, determined to look forward, not back.

Maria turned to give him a glowing smile. 'And to you, Chico,' she insisted proudly. 'Without you none of us would be working in this world-class facility.'

He watched fondly as Maria busied herself filing the letter away with all her other treasured possessions, as she referred to the many letters of praise they received.

'As soon as we receive the official certificate I'm going to have it framed and hung on the wall with the rest,' she told him proudly.

'And I'm going to treat you and the staff to a party to celebrate, and thank you all for everything you've done for me, Maria.' He gave her a hug.

'We've come a long way together, Chico.'

As he released Maria and stepped back he could see in her eyes that Maria was thinking how easily Chico could have taken a very different path. His road out of the gutter had begun the day he wandered into Eduardo's recruitment rally by mistake. Another do-gooder, he'd thought scornfully, contemptuous of the rapt faces all around him. He had believed Eduardo to be one of the rich pigs that came to hand out largesse in the slums to make themselves feel better. Soft *bastardo!* he'd thought viciously. Ten years old and all fired up, he had been on his way to confront the drug pushers who had killed his brother and Maria's son, with a loaded gun stuck into his belt and murder on his mind. Eduardo must have seen something of this in his eyes and had called him forward. Chico had remained stubbornly planted, but Eduardo wasn't so easy to refuse, and Eduardo was big, and hard, and firm, though Chico could still remember shooting venom from his eyes when Eduardo took a firm hold of him. He hated authority. What had authority done for him? Where were the police when his brother was shot? He hated the privilege that brought individuals like Eduardo sightseeing to the *barrio* and bought rich boys out of trouble. And he hated Eduardo for no better reason than the esteemed polo player was trespassing on Chico's territory, confronting issues Chico was so sure Eduardo couldn't understand. But Eduardo had his arm in an iron grip, and his gun was soon in Eduardo's pocket. There would be no murders committed that day.

'I owe it all to you and to Eduardo, Maria,' he said now. 'Everything I have is because you two believed in me.'

'And we weren't wrong, were we?' Maria planted her capable hands on her ample hips as she confronted him. 'Against all the odds, the poor boy from the *barrio* finds himself here.' She said this expansively, as if they lived in a palace, rather than on a ranch as she gestured around ecstatically with another of her beaming smiles.

His face softened too. How could it not? Every day he relished this life, for Maria's sake as much as his own. It couldn't have happened if Eduardo hadn't treated him like a son, believing in him, however hard Chico had made things for Eduardo. And Chico had made things hard, though he had idolised his mentor. He still couldn't believe how lucky he was, to have been chosen to work for such a famous polo player. Having taken him out of the *barrio*, Eduardo had shown him that there was so much more to life than drugs and guns and war, and when he'd died Eduardo had left Chico everything, knowing his devoted charge would pick up Eduardo's causes and infuse them with new life.

He had used the money Eduardo left him to buy and develop a hand-to-mouth scrub ranch, which after years of hard labour he had transformed from an unpromising stretch of land into the most prestigious polo centre in the world. He had accomplished this because he was meticulous and driven, and because, as Eduardo had noted, Chico had a special way with horses. This gift came from the early days of working for Eduardo, Chico believed. When he could confide in no one else the ponies listened to him, and in return they gave him their trust. This interaction between man and beast had led owners and players alike to think he had some special magic. There was no magic. Polo ponies were competitive and he gave them every reason to trust him, so they obeyed his smallest command. They trusted him to keep them safe and bring out the best in them. Women thought the same thing, but unlike the animals, he had no interest in wasting his time or his emotions on women.

'Chico…?' Maria prompted hesitantly, seeing he was lost in thought.

'Maria?' He gave her an encouraging smile.

'Would you like me to walk you through this year's intake of scholarship students?'

'No. Thank you, Maria, but I'll take the list with me, and study your report later.'

He didn't want anyone around when he did that, let alone the impressionable Maria. Reading that one name had been enough to make him feel as if his guts had been wrenched out and thrust down his throat, and he had to take a moment to control the emotion clawing at his senses that said someone would pay for this oversight.

Yes. He should pay. He should have checked this year's intake before he went on the polo tour, and then this would never have happened.

'Is something troubling you, Chico?' Maria asked him with concern.

'There's never enough time, Maria.' He half smiled as he said this, needing to put Maria off the scent. She could read him so easily after all these years of working closely together, and this was one occasion when he could do without her friendly advice. 'Don't look so worried,' he insisted as he took charge of the list. 'I trust my selection team, which is why I appointed them.'

'Of course, Chico,' the older woman agreed, her gaze sliding away from his, as if she was only halfway convinced.

He couldn't blame his team for this error. How were they supposed to know what had happened in his youth? People had only heard rumours. Even Maria didn't know everything. There were some things Chico would never share, not even with Maria.

His stomach clenched as he thought back to the day

Serena Fane had accused him of rape. It was a preposterous lie, but who would believe him, the poor boy from the slums of Brazil? He had stood no chance against the might of the British aristocracy. He had written to Lizzie on countless occasions after that first letter, begging for an explanation, so sure she'd write back. They'd been so close. She was the only young friend he'd ever had, and he'd trusted her completely. And, yes, she'd been beautiful, but Lizzie had been so far out of his reach, he had only dared to talk to her when she'd shown an interest in befriending him.

Rape was a word he'd associated with the murderers who had killed his brother, and his shock when Lizzie had ignored his letters begging her to clear his name was indescribable. He could only think that she had sided with *them*—her slutty mother and drunken father, whom he had guessed all along were only looking for 'hush money' from Eduardo. He had never discovered if any money had changed hands, as Eduardo would never speak of it, but he had his suspicions, especially as when Chico became headline news in the polo world Serena had reappeared, threatening to reopen the scandal if he didn't 'make her comfortable'.

He'd thrown her out, and had only baulked at bringing charges for blackmail against her because Lizzie's grandmother had been so good to him, and he didn't want to bring the old lady any more pain. Lizzie's grandmother was the only other person, apart from Eduardo, who had believed in him, and she had helped Eduardo get him away when Lord Fane had brought his scandalous charges at the behest of his wife. Chico always paid his debts, and he never forgot a slight, but if only Lizzie had had the courage to speak out at the time none of this would have happened.

And, yes, she was only fifteen at the time, but it was clear to him now that their friendship had meant nothing to her.

Too heated to remain in the office, he headed out to check the ranch. He did this every season when he returned from the polo circuit. It wasn't a quick job as his land extended to tens of thousands of acres these days and took a few weeks to inspect. There were preparations to make before he left. While his students were settling in, this was the best time for him to be away. There were other tutors who would take care of them and start their training while he was gone. When he came back he'd check Lady Elizabeth Fane out, to see what the hell Lizzie thought she was doing here. His best guess was that from interrogation to deportation would take a lot less time than inspecting his ranch.

CHAPTER TWO

'A COLD POULTICE was what you needed, wasn't it?' Stepping back, Lizzie took a long thoughtful look at the patient. She was relieved to see the pony was happy enough to start nosing a net of hay. 'That, and a bit of a chat,' she prescribed, stroking the polo pony's velvety ears. 'The swelling's gone down and you'll soon be back to your usual cantankerous self—answering back with a nip on the arm whenever I speak to you.'

'Do horses answer back?' Danny observed, throwing her arms wide on the hay. 'Can I have a cold poultice please? All over my body, if you've got one big enough? I'm boiling.'

It had been a long, hard working day for both girls, who had been bringing in horses from the outlying pastures, but Lizzie refused to acknowledge that it was time to stop work until she'd finished the job in hand. There was never an official clocking-off time for Lizzie where horses were concerned.

'It is hot,' she agreed. 'Would you like a mint?'

'I'd love one.'

Lizzie smiled at Danny. 'I'm talking to the horse.'

'Then, will you please stop talking to the horse,' Danny complained, 'and concentrate on me? I'm slowly melting here while you run your equine counselling service.'

'Here—' Lizzie tossed a tube of mints across for Danny to catch.

'Do you think we'll ever meet our leader?' Danny asked, cramming a handful of mints into her mouth. 'Personally, I'm beginning to doubt he exists.'

'We know he exists,' Lizzie said sensibly, wishing Danny hadn't brought up the subject of Chico Fernandez. 'He piloted the plane that brought us here.'

'So, where is he?' Danny demanded.

'I don't know. I'm in no hurry to see him. Are you?'

'Liar,' Danny accused. 'Your face has pinked up, and your eyes are huge. I'm not going into any further anatomical detail on the basis that it wouldn't be appropriate between friends. But, honestly, Lizzie, please don't ask me to believe that you're not eaten up with excitement at the thought of seeing Chico again.'

'That's where you're wrong. I blame Chico for my obsession with all things equine, and nothing else.' Which was also a lie, but Danny didn't need to know that.

'I remember,' Danny mused. 'Since the moment you met Chico, you talked of nothing but having a life with horses, just like him. And now here we are, on his training ranch,' she exclaimed.

Lizzie faked a laugh, wishing she could join in Danny's upbeat mood. True, everything on Fazenda Fernandez had surpassed her wildest expectation, and she was more determined than ever to excel and pass her diploma with top honours, but when it came to Chico...

'Suck him dry, Lizzie, and then take his ideas back to Scotland, so you can use them to set up in competition and destroy him.'

She didn't hate Chico as much as her father wished she did. In fact, she didn't hate him at all, but she did feel disillusioned by him. She couldn't even blame him if he had flirted with her mother, though she guessed Serena would be the instigator. Would Chico force himself on her mother? No. Would he rape her? Absolutely not. But Lizzie's mother was still a very attractive woman, and Chico had always been a free spirit. But he could have been straight with her instead of promising to rescue her from Rottingdean House, and then disappearing without a word.

'Share your thoughts,' Danny insisted, crunching mints noisily as she sprawled out on the hay.

Not a chance, Lizzie thought ruefully. In this instance, she wouldn't be confiding in her friend. 'Hang up the tack for me, and then we'll talk. It's steaming in here. I'm melting after moving all that hay.' Fanning herself, Lizzie started to peel off her breeches and claggy top. She relished the freedom of thong and sports bra for a few moments, before reaching for her jeans. 'The heat, when you've been working as hard as we have, certainly takes it out of you.'

'It's not the only thing that's hot,' Danny observed with mischief in her voice.

'The men?' Lizzie pretended disinterest. Wiping her arm across her glowing face, she bundled her bright copper hair up into a band.

Danny opened an eye. 'Don't pretend you haven't noticed them. The gauchos are off-the-scale hot, while the polo players are like gilt-edged invitations to sin.'

'Really?' Lizzie's lips pressed down. 'I can't say I've noticed.'

'Like hell you haven't,' Danny scoffed.

There was only one man Lizzie was interested in, and their paths hadn't even crossed yet. She guessed Chico must have been busy catching up with everything that had happened while he'd been away, and doubted he'd even recognise her when they met again. She was hardly fifteen years old now. Nor was she impressionable, or prone to having a crush on a man who looked like a barbarian, and who had the morals of a goat, according to the scandal sheets. It was hard to miss the bad boy of polo, as the sports pages called him, when Chico scored as many front covers on polo magazines as he'd scored goals this season.

Leaning her head back against the wall of the stall with her arms outstretched, she relished the breeze coming in from an open window on her naked skin. 'Do you think anyone's going to notice if I just forget to put on my top?'

'Who's going to see you?' Danny pointed out. 'There's only one horse in the stable block, and we're his grooms.'

Lizzie relaxed as her friend hefted the horse's saddle over her arm, and picked up his bridle. Danny was right. Who was going to see her?

Coltish limbs and an intriguing flash of naked skin held him motionless for a moment as the girl struggled to pull on a fresh top over what appeared to be—at least to her, judging by her muttered curses—inconveniently large breasts. He wanted to check on a pony that had suffered a bad knock during a match while he'd been away. The pony's spirit would benefit from human contact and he was keen to make sure it was as comfortable as possible. Anyone who believed animals couldn't understand what was said to them was missing an empathy gene, in his opinion. He had heard the two female grooms talking, but one of them had left the stall and slipped out of the back entrance that led to the tack room where they stowed their gear. Grooms hanging round so late in the day were either up to no good, or were working late, which meant one of two things: they were dross he'd get rid of, or they were the best of the best. He was keen to find out which category he was dealing with. Shouldering a pitchfork to make the hay bed in the stall more comfortable for the horse, he grabbed a fistful of pony nuts and strolled down the line of stalls.

Emotion caught him square in the gut as a halo of red-gold curls gave the groom's identity away. He would have known her anywhere, even after all these years. The half-naked body belonged to Lizzie Fane. Perfect.

'Out of there, now,' he rapped.

'What?' a girl who sounded in no way dismayed demanded. 'Who is this?'

It was a shock to hear adult Lizzie sounding just like her mother. Not good.

'I said,' he repeated in a menacing tone, 'get out of there now.'

'Do you mind?' she replied in the same honeyed voice. 'Your tone is upsetting the horse.'

She had a nerve. No one cared about horses more than he did.

Had he really imagined he would know how it felt to be confronted by a member of the Fane family on his *fazenda*? He'd been nowhere close. Anger consumed him as the past rushed back. The humiliation he'd suffered—the expense to Eduardo, thanks to the false accusations made against Chico, and the fact that Lizzie had turned her back on him.

'I won't be a minute,' she murmured.

Was he supposed to wait?

'There are some things I need to pick up and put away,' she explained, still in the same mild voice, and still mostly hidden from him in the stall.

'The clock's ticking,' he warned, gritting out each word.

He rested against the wall, thinking back to when he'd

been a youth and an easy target for two cheats with their eyes on the money of his sponsor, Eduardo Delgardo. Lies about him forcing himself on Serena Fane, Lizzie's mother, had tripped so easily off their tongues. Even Eduardo had been hard-pressed to defend him, though the older man had remained his staunchest defender throughout, and had explained, once they were safely back in Brazil, that Lizzie's grandmother had discovered the truth about the life her son and his wife were leading, and that when they used Chico to try and get money out of Eduardo, it was the last straw for the old lady, who had disinherited her son, and banished both him and his wife from Rottingdean House. Unfortunately, by this time, Lord and Lady Fane had stolen all her money.

For a man to steal money from his mother was incomprehensible to Chico, but he had soon realised that men like Lizzie's father had no conscience. And now that man's daughter was here on a scholarship, working towards a diploma, which he would award? You couldn't make it up.

'What are you waiting for?' he snarled as the past blinded him with an angry red mist. He'd waited long enough. Switching on the overhead light, he bathed them both in stark white light, and, lifting the latch, he walked in.

The man she'd called her friend was right behind her. Smouldering, powerful, different. The Deceiver. The Liar. The youth who had told her that he understood how it must be for her living at Rottingdean House with parents who ignored her, and had promised to take her away. He had failed to deliver on that promise, and her forgiving nature was out of the door. Her body responded eagerly to the hard man of polo before she'd even turned around, but her thoughts were filled with anger and disappointment in the man she had once believed was her friend.

She would have to master those feelings, if she was going to complete the course, Lizzie told herself firmly. And with a muttered apology, she straightened up and turned around.

Light shimmered around Chico, pointing up his darkness. She couldn't breathe for a moment. His glittering menace had never seemed more pronounced. As she had first suspected when she caught a glimpse of him on the plane, Chico was vastly changed. This wasn't the ridiculously good-looking youth with the easy smile and relaxed manner, but a hard, driven man, whom life had made suspicious, a man with single-minded determination that had taken Chico Fernandez to the top. That didn't stop her body burning with lust. Her reaction to him was primal. She had no defence against it. Her mind was scrambled, and yet she was acutely aware of him. Forbidden fruit had never looked this good.

All the more reason to keep her head down and get back to the job, Lizzie reasoned. There were always things to do in the stable, and she was here to accomplish something crucial for the future of Rottingdean, not to rehash the mistakes of the past. She might never be exactly sure what had happened all those years ago, but she knew what she had to do to secure the future of Rottingdean now, and make things right for everyone who worked on the estate, and that didn't include falling like some heartsick teenager for a man who had proved conclusively that he cared nothing for her.

Lizzie was bending over with her back to him, loading pots of salve and rolls of bandage into a carrying case. His glance swept over her. Lizzie Fane was all grown up. Long limbs, slender frame, generous hips, and still the same bright red wavy hair, longer than he remembered, and carelessly swept back and bundled into a glowing topknot with strands and curls escaping everywhere. He closed his mind to her attractions, and ground his jaw as the seconds ticked by. The least she could do was acknowledge her boss.

'Sorry,' she said, sounding not the least bit repentant, and looking even less so. 'I had to finish what I was doing.'

He hummed as heat ripped through him, and it was a surprise to find the connection between them was as strong as ever, even after all this time. Once they had been drawn together by mutual curiosity—two people from very different backgrounds, both outsiders in their own way, with only horses in common, but now it was a hot-blooded man, and a beautiful, if icy woman, weighing each other up like prize-fighters from opposite sides of the ring.

'It's good to see you again,' Lizzie announced in a businesslike way.

He replied to this with a steady look. The connection might be there, but they were strangers, he thought, and the steel in Lizzie's eyes intrigued him. She had always been a tomboy, but there was something in her expression now that suggested she was still hurting because he'd let her down by leaving Rottingdean House all those years ago without saying goodbye. Had he meant so much to her?

When he was least expecting it, she relaxed and smiled. 'I'm really pleased to be here.'

Now he was confused. What was he to believe? Lizzie with a grudge? Or Lizzie, the student determined to impress? She had always been good at hiding her feelings. She'd had to be. There was only one certainty here. The power of her stunning emerald gaze had hit him like a punch in the gut.

What was wrong with him? He shook her hand, and

now he didn't want to let her go? To feel her hand in his grip, so small, so slender, so cool, had made him want to ask her straight out: what happened to you? To us? Worse, he had to fight the crazy impulse to drag her close and kiss her hard.

'It's been a long time, Lizzie,' he said finally with commendable restraint.

'It has,' she agreed coolly. 'I'm sorry I kept you waiting, but I had to be sure I'd picked everything up, and that Flame was properly settled for the night.'

He inspected the work she'd done on the horse. She'd done a good job, but not good enough to meet his exacting standards. He'd pulled Lizzie's report from her college. She'd passed out top of her class, which was why she had been awarded the scholarship to train under him at Fazenda Fernandez. He remembered her grandmother telling him that Lizzie needed something to lose herself in. He had understood immediately that Lizzie found the affection denied her by her parents from the horses she cared for, because he'd found that same solace, but what was driving her now?

'Well, if that's all?' she said pleasantly.

She waited patiently for him to move out of the way. She had inherited none of the supercilious qualities of her parents, he noted, but her eyes were wounded. The past had damaged them both, but why had she chosen to believe her parents' lies over him? The answer came to him as they stared at each other. However a child was misled or mistreated, they never gave up hope of winning the love of their parent, even if that parent was incapable of giving love.

'You have a wonderful facility here, Senhor Fernandez. I'm thrilled to have been given the opportunity to train here.'

She was close enough to touch, to kiss, to reassure…

'And we're very glad to have you here,' he replied in the same measured tone. 'You come with an excellent recommendation from your college.'

She smiled in response to this, and tension crackled all around them, making him wonder if they would ever be easy with each other again.

'Anyway, thank you,' she said, breaking the spell as she hefted her belongings into a more comfortable position. 'I really do appreciate the chance you've given me.'

'My selection team did that. Everything I do here is in honour of my sponsor, Eduardo. You do remember Eduardo?'

'Yes, of course I do.' For a moment her confident mask slipped. 'I was very sorry to hear of his passing. I read quite a lot about him before I came here.'

'Oh?'

'When you both came to Rottingdean I just knew him as a leading polo player in Brazil. What I didn't realise was that Eduardo had devoted himself to providing education for children from deprived backgrounds.'

'Children like me?'

'Yes.' She held his gaze, unflinching. 'I don't say that to offend you, Senhor Fernandez.'

'I appreciate your honesty, Senhorita Fane.'

She slanted him a thoughtful look and almost smiled again. 'I guess Eduardo got lucky with you.'

'There are many deserving children,' he argued sharply as their hopeful faces flashed into his mind.

Lizzie blushed bright red. 'I realise that—I didn't mean…I just meant—'

'I know what you meant. You're wondering how I can afford all this?' Not by cheating like Lizzie's parents, that was for sure.

'No,' she protested, and for the first time he thought he saw the real Lizzie, rather than the girl who was trying to please her boss. 'It makes perfect sense to me. With your natural talent you were always bound to succeed.'

'And you also realised that success such as mine pays well?' he pressed, thinking of her mother and wondering if Lizzie had inherited any of Serena's acquisitive traits.

'Your financial success is well documented,' she defended, her cheeks pinking up again beneath his suspicious stare.

Was she after a slice of the pie? 'Hard work and straight dealing is my only secret.'

'And a sponsor like Eduardo,' she suggested, that steel he'd seen before returning to her gaze.

Even now, hearing Eduardo's name coming from a member of the Fane family's lips grated on him, though he had to admit that the fact Lizzie had no problem speaking up for herself was to her credit. Her parents had always delivered their barbs from a safe distance.

'I'm in awe of the legacy Eduardo Delgardo left behind, and I don't just mean his money,' she explained. 'He inspired so many people with his good works, including me.'

Her steady gaze convinced him that in this, at least, Lizzie Fane was being totally honest.

'I should go to supper now. My friend's expecting me—' She started to move past him.

He wasn't ready to let her go yet and stood in her way. 'You bandaged him?'

'Yes?' Her concern was obvious.

'Put your things down outside the stable, and come back in here.' Her eyes widened. 'Back in here,' he repeated.

He was already hunkering down to check the poultice when she returned to the stall. Apart from wanting to show Lizzie how her bandaging technique could be improved, and disregarding the obvious questions jostling in his mind, he was intrigued by this new Lizzie. Forget intrigue. He wanted her. In the past he had put her on a pedestal and wouldn't have touched her. But now...

CHAPTER THREE

COULDN'T THIS WAIT? There were classes tomorrow. What did Chico really want? He was such a compelling presence he made her feel tongue-tied. Her lips felt wooden and when she tried to speak her voice sounded hoarse. Seeing him again after all these years had completely thrown her. Had she really thought she was ready for this? Just because Chico Fernandez had been the stuff of her fantasies throughout all her teenage years, didn't mean she knew him. She was keenly aware that she didn't know him, not now, which was why she felt so awkward around him—and nothing could dilute the impact of a man dressed in nothing more than a pair of banged-up jeans and a black top that showed off his impressive muscles, who had turned from an attractive youth into the hottest thing on two powerful male legs.

'It's hot in here, isn't it?' she said, finding it hard to breathe suddenly.

'Not overly so,' Chico replied. 'The temperature in here is controlled.'

Unlike her heart, she thought, feeling the effects of being trapped in a small stall with so much undiluted sex. Chico's physical presence was overwhelming. Shoulders broad enough to hoist an ox, stomach flat, waist slim, from all his exercise on horseback—and, when he was hunkered down like this, a grandstand view of the tightest butt on earth. Added to which, a heavy-duty leather belt was drawing her gaze where it definitely shouldn't wander. And his face—if Helen of Troy could launch a thousand ships, Chico Fernandez could launch a thousand erotic fantasies. He looked so stern, but his mouth was the mouth of a sensualist, and she loved his sharp black stubble. She had always loved his thick, wild black hair—

What was she thinking? She wasn't a naïve girl now, daydreaming in the stables at Rottingdean. She was a woman with a goal, who had won a scholarship to Brazil, and who couldn't afford to be distracted. What must she look like to Chico? Hot, sweaty, and grubby— Quite suddenly, she didn't have confidence in anything—not in herself, or her work, or her future. This wasn't the youth she had made a friend of all those years ago. This was Chico Fernandez, acknowledged equine expert—and expert between the sheets too, she had no doubt; a man with testosterone flying off him like white-hot shards that pierced her body with sensation until she couldn't think. Chico was said to be a man's man; a lone wolf who ruled his territory like a feudal lord. Was she here to take *him* on? Was *she* going to suck *him* dry?

'Not a bad job,' he remarked, glancing up at her.

'Really?' The last thing she had been expecting from him was words of praise.

'But not good enough for the standards we set here. That's why you've come to train at Fazenda Fernandez, isn't it, Lizzie?'

There was a flash of suspicion in his eyes, and for a moment she had no idea why she was here, only that she was mad to have come. Echoes from the past came back to haunt her—snatches of conversation, that she had barely understood as a young teen.

'Are you listening, Lizzie? If you don't pay attention, you'll learn nothing.'

She shook herself round. 'I'm sorry.'

'If you intend to stay on here and complete the training—'

'I will complete the training.'

Chico's eyes sparked as he sprang up to confront her. A clash of wills was the last thing she had intended, but she had never learned how to admit defeat, and she was determined to achieve all her goals here, including keeping Chico Fernandez at arm's length.

She regretted her outburst when she saw Chico's expression turn cold. She would have to keep her feelings closely guarded in future.

'You will attend my tutorial here, tomorrow morning, at six a.m. sharp,' he said without a hint of warmth.

'Yes. Of course.'

Her best guess was, Chico didn't think she'd last the course, and he was notorious for failing students who didn't make the grade. There were no second chances— except for Danny, who had somehow managed to get her heart broken by a polo player, and had been allowed to go home and restart this year.

From confronting him, she was thrown back into pleading her cause. 'I just want to do my best for every horse.'

'I would expect nothing less of one of my students.'

He moved at the same time she did. They almost collided in the middle of the stall. He was close enough for her to smell the soap on his skin and the sunshine in his clothes, and the warmth of his impossibly powerful body, which was far, far, far too close for safety. Some of the buttons on his shirt were open, revealing tanned, hard-muscled skin—

'When you're ready?'

Chico's voice was low and strummed her senses as she moved aside. He held her fate in the palm of his hand, yet her body was melting with want, which was insane, and absolutely the last thing she needed. She had to keep a clear head if she was going to achieve anything here, and being reduced to a mass of hormones was hardly going to help her do that.

'Don't let me keep you from your supper.'

There was a faint mocking note in his voice as if he knew the effect his brutal masculinity could have on even the most reluctant target.

'Until tomorrow at six a.m.,' she confirmed, taking care to keep her voice on the pleasant side of neutral.

She left the stall in a rush, and didn't stop until she reached the tack room, where she stowed the medical supplies and then leaned back with her eyes closed and her body pressed up hard against the cool wall until finally she could breathe.

On her way from the courtyard to the cookhouse, she wished she could bind her breasts, or become a boy—lose these feelings, anyway. How was she supposed to stay here with so many dangerous fantasies in her head? She'd thought she'd got it all worked out and would be prepared for seeing Chico again. Not even close. Seeing him again had only confused her more. His eyes had assessed her, warmed her and heated her blood to the point where all she could think about was sex. And there was no way on earth she would ever sleep with him. Boss and groom was bad enough, tutor and student was forbidden territory, but everything that had happened in the past— all those rumours—made her thoughts taboo. And even if the past hadn't stood between them—Chico Fernandez and Lizzie Fane? It could never happen. He was successful, famous, and rich, and she was no one. The only reason she was here was because she'd won a scholarship, and because her grandmother had insisted Lizzie must take up that scholarship, because an endorsement from Chico Fernandez was second to none.

And how did Chico feel about that?

Lizzie's heart thundered with apprehension. If she didn't make the grade, or he threw her out, who would save Rottingdean then?

'Hey—wait up. You forgot something…'

She turned, and her heart went into overdrive when she saw the grubby top she'd discarded in the stall, hanging from the tip of Chico's finger.

'Rule one,' he said, strolling up to her. 'Never leave anything in a stable that could harm your horse.'

She was mortified. She never did. She never had before. She'd slung the top over the top of the partition between the stalls, meaning to take it with her.

Seeing Chico again had knocked everything out of her head. The sheer force of his personality swamped her as she took the top. Chico Fernandez was one of life's primal forces, while she must look like the primmest thing on earth to him in her crisp white blouse, with its ironed and starched Peter Pan collar, her fresh-out-of-the-box sneakers, and her neatly pressed jeans. She had loved the outfit when she first put it on, because it was a parting gift from her grandmother. To bring her luck, Lizzie's grandmother had said. And she still loved the clothes, but she had to admit they were more garden party than gaucho. Almost in defiance of that, her nipples were tightening and her heart was thundering out of control. She grabbed the chance to take a deep, calming breath as he paused to turn and talk to one of his fellow polo players.

'Black eyes, black colours for his team, and a black heart has never stood in the way for Chico Fernandez

*when it comes to unparalleled Gaucho Polo success for
this world-beater...'* This quote from one of the articles she
had read about him seemed so relevant now. If Chico's opponents on the polo field were subject to this same force
field, no wonder they found him formidable. Most sports
commentators said there had never been a player like him.

And what did most women say?

She didn't even want to think about his other women.
She guessed Chico accepted what was freely offered and
then moved on, and could only thank her lucky stars that
fate had decreed she would never be one of his discards.

What a great thought—such a sensible thought—that
unfortunately had no influence on her body, and her body
still wanted him. She blamed it on the primal imperative
to mate with the leader of the pack.

'Forgive me,' Chico said brusquely, spinning round.
'Before you go to supper, I have one or two more questions for you, Lizzie.'

She felt the blood drain from her face. 'Oh?'

'As a representative of the grooms, could you tell me,
are your quarters comfortable?'

Why did he care? Was he trying to trip her up? Was he
looking for an excuse to get rid of her? 'Quite comfortable, thank you.'

He stabbed a glance at the utilitarian block where the
students were housed. What could she possibly have to
complain about? There was running water—possibly gla-
cier melt judging by the temperature—and she shared her
room with five other girls. No problem there. Only three of
them snored. And thanks to the freezing water they were
all quick in the shower.

'Your bed's comfortable?'

She frowned. 'Yes.'

She would have gladly slept on a bed of nails for the

chance to work at Fazenda Fernandez with the best trainer
in the world on the best polo ponies in the world, and she
really didn't want to discuss her sleeping arrangements
with Chico Fernandez. Was he determined to unsettle her?

'Thank you, Lizzie. I had thought of making some improvements to the grooms' accommodation, but I can now
see that that isn't necessary.'

Not necessary? Inwardly, she groaned. Imagine how
popular this was going to make her.

And then Chico stopped dead and she almost crashed
into him. His eyes narrowed as he stared down at her.
'Enjoy your supper, Lizzie.'

'I will.'

'Perhaps I'll see you later—'

Not if she could help it. She was going to stick to the
original plan—keep her head down, work hard, do well,
and then go home with her diploma and her pride intact,
so she could set up a viable business. What was so attractive about a snarl and a swagger, anyway?

He couldn't rest. The past wasn't just back, it had punched
him in the face, and he wasn't in the mood for the rau-
cous good humour of the cookhouse. He didn't want to
see anyone, talk to anyone, especially Lizzie Fane, and so
he paced the vast, polished oak floor on the ground floor
of his home as he tried to make sense of his feelings. He
paused by the window where he could see across the yard
to the cookhouse. What was she doing? Who was she with?
He wasn't fooled by her circumspect manner. Lizzie had
turned her back on him once. When he was of no further
use to her, would she do so again?

Probably, if he gave her the chance, which he wouldn't.

So was Lizzie Fane a force to be reckoned with? He
smiled at the thought of testing her out, but past events at

Rottingdean stood between them. He couldn't remember that time without being forced to accept that Lizzie had a damaged bloodline. Her father, Lord Reginald Fane, had been a dissolute pervert who beat his wife, while Lizzie's mother had been a liar and a cheat. Only Lizzie's grandmother, the Grand Duchess, had stood out like a beacon of light, but how much influence had the old lady brought to bear on Lizzie? Judging by Lizzie's contempt for his many letters to her, very little, he guessed.

Horses were easier to breed than people, he concluded. You could be sure of a horse's bloodline and its flaws. He'd been lucky that Eduardo had saved him, lifting him from the *barrio* like a drowning puppy in a sack in the river. Eduardo hadn't just taught him everything Chico knew about horses, but how to live and work responsibly, and how to care for his fellow human beings. He'd taught him how to eat in a civilised manner, and how to behave in society. Losing Eduardo had been like losing a father— a good father.

Learning Eduardo had left him everything had been the biggest shock of his life. Eduardo's last words had been to beg Chico to shrug off his past and learn from it, but how was he supposed to do that now that Lizzie Fane was back in his life? Leaving Lizzie twelve years ago had torn him up inside. How could they leave a fifteen-year-old child in the care of her nymphomaniac mother, and a violent, debauched father? he had asked Eduardo. He hadn't known then what they had accused him of, or why Eduardo and Lizzie's grandmother had been in such a hurry to get him away. He could still remember clutching his head as he raged about Lizzie's situation for the whole of their journey back to Brazil.

'It's not your job to save Lizzie,' Eduardo had told him firmly. 'You have your career to think about, and

Lord Fane is too powerful, too respected, for you to take him on.'

'But I will one day,' Chico had vowed.

'No,' Eduardo had told him flatly. 'You will forget this and keep your mind on your work and your future career. And as far as Lizzie Fane is concerned, you will forget her too, and place your trust, as I have done, in Lizzie's grandmother.'

Trust, he remembered agonising in mutinous teenage silence. What was that?

He knew now that trust was one of the most important parts of loving someone, and that Eduardo had trusted him like a son.

'So?' Danny demanded as she waited with Lizzie in the supper queue. 'What happened with Chico?'

Lizzie flashed a glance around.

'I don't know why you're being so secretive. I saw you walking across the yard with him—everyone must have…'

'Doesn't this smell delicious?' Lizzie remarked, refusing to rise to the bait. She and Danny were standing in front of the open grill where three chefs were preparing everything from vegetarian specials to man-sized steaks.

'Your attempt to change the subject has fallen on deaf ears, Lizzie Fane,' Danny assured her.

There were too many grooms around, as well as Chico's fellow polo players, for Lizzie to be indiscreet, but Danny wasn't going to let the subject drop. 'So, what do you want to know?' Lizzie asked.

'You were a long time alone with Chico, and so I was wondering…'

'He was telling me about the bandaging tutorial we have to attend at six tomorrow morning.'

As Danny groaned the polo player behind them, muddy

and with his hair tousled from a game, exclaimed, 'Wake up and move along, will you? Hungry people are waiting to be fed here.'

'Calm down, man mountain,' Danny flashed, rounding on him. 'We're hungry too.'

'Then hurry up and choose your food, fresh meat—'

'Watch it, nuts for brains, or it'll be your meat on the grill,' Danny fired back.

'I love your ladylike way with words,' Lizzie murmured as the good-looking guy stared down at Danny with amusement.

'Are you all like this back home?' he demanded, directing the question at Danny.

'Believe it,' Danny snapped, exchanging an appreciative look with Lizzie.

'Tiago,' Lizzie confirmed in a discreet murmur. 'One of the top players. You must have seen him on the cover of *Polo Times*? Bad. Very bad.'

'Excellent,' Danny mouthed.

'That's your Christmas present sorted.'

'Promise?'

'It's a deal,' Lizzie confirmed.

Danny was about to say something smart back, but her words choked off abruptly when she saw the expression on Lizzie's face. Nothing more needed to be said. Chico Fernandez had just walked into the cookhouse.

CHAPTER FOUR

LIZZIE DIDN'T NEED to look at Chico to know he was there when she could feel him in every fibre of her being. Determined not be distracted by the sudden overload of testosterone, she calmly gave her order to the chef. 'Tomatoes, eggplant, fries, and—'

'And the biggest steak you've got,' a husky male voice interrupted.

Having casually jumped the queue, Chico was handed a plate already loaded with every delicacy his uniformed chefs could provide. 'I don't want my new recruits fainting on the job,' he explained. 'Here—take this.' He pressed his own plate of food into Lizzie's hands. 'Well?' he demanded impatiently. 'Don't stand there staring at it. Eat before it gets cold.'

'I'm a vegetarian.'

'Vegan?'

'No.'

'Slap a hunk of cheese onto her plate,' he ordered the chefs, swapping plates.

Lizzie passed the plate forward to the waiting chef. 'Cheese omelette, please.'

Damn, if she didn't sound like the prissiest food freak on the planet, but no way was she being told what she could eat. Chico Fernandez might rule what she did as a

student, but her downtime was her own. Tilting her chin
at a determined angle, she joined Danny at a table by the
window where they could chat undisturbed—only to discover that Danny, like everyone else in the cookhouse,
had been watching Lizzie's exchange with Chico with interest. Didn't anyone *ever* take him on? Lizzie wondered.

'Do you have to provoke him?' Danny demanded.

'Why not? It's fun. I had to stand up to him. Dinosaur—
trying to make me eat his plate of flesh.' She flashed a
glance at Chico's table, knowing it was more than Chico's
dietary concerns for her. These brief encounters with him
were bringing it all back to her—the times they'd shared,
the jokes they'd told, the gossip they'd exchanged, and
the wild rides they'd enjoyed through the magical glens
of Scotland. And weighted against that—very heavily
weighted against that—was the pain he'd caused her, and
that was like a reopened wound as if Chico deserting her
had only happened yesterday. She'd gone downstairs on
the morning he left to find all the other grooms in the stable yard at Rottingdean, but no sign of Chico. She could
still feel the sickening blow of incredulity when they told
her he'd gone back to Brazil with Eduardo. She couldn't
believe them—and now? Looking back, she had to admit
her feelings all those years ago had been the overreaction
of a hormonal teenage girl.

'Fun?' Danny queried, breaking into her thoughts. 'If
that's what you look like when you're having fun, I'd hate
to see you when you're angry.'

'Sorry.' Shaking her head as if that could disperse the
memories, she set about distracting Danny. 'You weren't
exactly all sweetness and light with Tiago, I seem to re-
call.'

'And where's the similarity in that?' Danny asked, paus-
ing with her fork halfway to her mouth. 'One polo player

owns this facility and can throw us both out on a whim, while the other is a guest player. Chico is a whole different deal. You know that as well as I do, Lizzie, and you shouldn't take him on. Just behave,' Danny coaxed as Lizzie pretended nothing was wrong as she tucked into her omelette.

'I promise,' Lizzie agreed.

'For how long?' Danny groaned as she followed Lizzie's gaze.

'Hateful man,' Lizzie muttered as Chico raised his glass to her.

'I can see how much you hate him,' Danny remarked as Lizzie's cheeks flamed red.

Bandaging. Something Lizzie had believed she could do really well, but maybe not at six o' clock in the morning. The class had gathered round Chico to pay attention as he worked, while all she could register was that his touch was so deft, that watching those long, lean fingers was a thought-stealing distraction—

'Lizzie?' Chico glanced up. 'Would you care to demonstrate my technique to the class, please?'

This would be all right if she could concentrate, and if her cheeks didn't burn red from Chico being so close to her. She actually gasped when their stares met and held. 'Sorry—I'm being fumble-fingered this morning.'

'No problem,' Chico growled. 'We can wait.'

And she did make a good job of it. 'Same time tomorrow, everyone,' Chico said when she'd finished.

Straightening up, she turned to leave with the other grooms, but Chico stopped her with his hand on her arm. Relax, she told herself firmly as heat zigzagged through her.

'I know what you're thinking,' he began.

She sincerely hoped not. Her thoughts were the wrong side of X-rated.

'You think I'm being hard on you, for no good reason, but either you want to succeed or you don't.'

'I want to be the best,' she said frankly.

'Good.' Chico's level stare held her gaze, and she got the uncomfortable feeling that somehow he could read her thoughts. 'I know you from way back, Lizzie, and if you build on the talent you showed then, you could be the best.'

'Thank you.'

She left the stall thoughtfully, half hoping he would call her back. It would have been good to talk as they had used to, but that was another one of her daydreams, and Chico had no trouble separating their personal and professional lives. If only she could do the same. The air had been electric between them with so much left unsaid. Perhaps it was better that way, though she had a suspicion that at some point they would have to clear the air between them, and that it might be explosive when it happened, with years of bottled-up emotions on both sides pouring out.

He leaned back against the dividing wall of the stall, thinking about Lizzie, and wondering why fate had seen fit to reunite them. Lizzie's wildflower scent was in his head, but what did she feel about him? Guilt? Regret? She wasn't easy to read. What did she remember about all those years ago? Why hadn't she responded to his letters? He could accept that her parents would tell her lies about him, but Lizzie knew him—or she had used to.

No child would willingly believe a stranger above her own parents, he reasoned, but Lizzie was a woman now, and surely she had worked out what type of people they were?

Yes, life should be simple, and fate should stay out of

it, but, whatever happened while Lizzie was on his course, the next few months should prove instructive—for both of them.

Chico Fernandez, Lizzie fumed as she crossed the yard on her way to the cookhouse for breakfast. How was she ever going to get that man out of her head? She couldn't think of anything else. She hadn't slept a wink last night, because her head was full of him—full of sex. She had come here with one goal in mind, and now she had another, more pressing preoccupation—sex. Danny hadn't helped, saying there was nothing wrong with being a healthy female with healthy female urges.

If only it were that simple! If only she could get through the day without being in what could only be described as a heightened state of sexual arousal, which precluded having a sensible thought in her head. So, what did this mean? Was she going to be incapable of functioning until she'd had sex with Chico Fernandez? Couldn't she be stronger than that?

And, if she did have sex with him, what then?

Her heart would be broken. Her nights would be even more troubled, and she would probably be thrown off the course.

Great. Were Chico's nights troubled? Somehow, she doubted it.

'There's a letter for you, Lizzie,' Danny said as soon as Lizzie had settled into her chair at what had become their regular table by the window.

It was a letter from home. All thoughts of Chico temporarily suspended, her heart raced as she opened the envelope. She hated having to leave her grandmother to face their many creditors alone, and dreaded what the letter contained.

'So?' Danny prompted.

'So…?' Lizzie repeated distractedly as she scanned the letter quickly.

'So yet again, you were hanging out with the man of the moment for a long time, so I just wondered—'

'Well, stop wondering, because nothing happened.' Lizzie looked up and then read through the letter again, slowly this time.

'Not bad news, I hope?' Danny prompted.

Lizzie shook her head. 'I'll get us both some coffee, shall I?'

Danny stared after her with concern as she got up from her chair and walked out of the cookhouse. She needed a moment to think—time alone to gather her thoughts. Her grandmother had become gradually weaker; the doctor thought it advisable for her to spend a little time in hospital. The house would be locked up, and everything would be safe, so there was nothing for Lizzie to worry about— which made Lizzie wonder if there was anything she could have read to worry her more. Whatever happened, nothing must be allowed to get in the way of the course, her grandmother had written in her shaking script. Lizzie had to save the family firm. *'There's no one else, Lizzie. There's only you left now.'*

'Can you move away from the door, please? You're holding up some hungry men.'

She looked up with a start, straight into Chico's cool, assessing stare.

'I'm sorry—' She lurched out of his way, only to have him steady her and steer her back inside the cookhouse.

She made her way distractedly back to the table.

'Where's the coffee? Never mind,' Danny said, seeing Lizzie's face. 'I'll get us some.'

Lizzie sank into the chair, feeling extremely vulnerable

and a long way from home. Her grandmother had always been the lynchpin of her life, and she loved her without qualification. The letter was preparing her for a truth that Lizzie would never be ready to face. How could she stay on here now, as her grandmother had asked her to? How could she concentrate knowing her grandmother was so ill? Why had she ever imagined she could stick it out here while all this was going on at home?

'What's the matter?' Danny said as soon as she came back to the table. 'Did Chico say something to upset you?'

Lizzie shook her head.

'So it's the letter from home that's upsetting you,' Danny guessed.

'Yes—I'm sorry, Danny—'

'But your breakfast—'

'I just need a minute—'

Chico stood back as she barged out of the cookhouse. Running blindly across the yard, she didn't stop until she reached Flame's stall where she hunkered down in a corner to bury her head in her knees to think. She should go home. That was where she was needed most. But she had to stay to earn that diploma to hang in the office of the business she was going to rebuild. Without that accreditation, she was no use to anyone. *What to do? What to do—?*

'Lizzie?'

'Chico!' She sprang up, pressing herself against the wall between the stalls as he slipped the latch and walked in.

'If this course is too much for you—'

'It isn't,' she said, recovering fast.

'Then, what is the matter with you?' He glanced at the letter in her hand. 'Not bad news from home, I hope? Your grandmother?' he prompted with concern.

Not for the first time, he had disarmed her with his human side. It was easier to deal with the hard, unforgiving man than this. The fact that Chico still cared about her grandmother brought tears to her eyes, and she hated herself for the weakness, but, like it or not, Chico was a link between here and home. He knew her grandmother. He remembered what a special lady she was.

She mustn't show weakness. She had to be strong. She owed it to her grandmother to leave Chico Fernandez in no doubt that, whatever happened, she wasn't going anywhere until she finished his course.

'If you need to go home—'

'I don't,' she said firmly. Decision made, she stuffed the letter into her pocket. 'You may not think I've made the best of starts, but I can and will improve—'

'Lizzie.' The faintest of smiles tugged at one corner of his mouth. 'You're doing really well, but we have a waiting list if you do want to drop out?'

'I don't want to drop out. And I'm only too well aware of how many candidates would love to take my place.'

Chico held up his hands to calm her. 'Then, may I suggest you relax and make the most of your time here?'

How close they'd been, she thought as a wave of wistfulness swept over her, and how far apart they were now. How fierce was her urge to hug him tightly and share her fears about her grandmother with someone who would understand, but there was a barrier between them that prevented her doing so. Perhaps the past would always stand between them.

Lizzie looked so vulnerable that he was tempted to soften, but then he remembered that the line of strong characters in the Fane family had skipped a generation. Had they skipped another with Lizzie?

'If there's a problem I expect you to tell me,' he said in his firm tutor's voice. 'If money's a problem, or you're worried about your grandmother, I'll buy you a plane ticket home.'

'Thank you for the offer, but it's not necessary.' She tipped her chin up to stare him in the eyes.

He stepped in her way, one hand resting on the wall of the stall to stop her. He felt vaguely nettled. Why did she always have to do things alone? 'Just let me know if things change.'

'I will,' she assured him stiffly, not giving one inch.

Losing patience, he put his hand on her arm to move her aside. She was warm, firm, tempting, but that stubbornness was irreversible.

He followed her out, closing the stable door behind them, and then followed Lizzie down the line of stalls. He could see her concern for her grandmother in the tension in her back. He sensed she was holding back tears. Well, if she wouldn't let him, he couldn't help her. He supposed too much dirty water had flowed beneath the bridge for either of them to ever trust each other again. That thought riled him. He didn't like being shut out.

He was merciless with his students during that morning's training. Pushing them to the limits of their endurance, he made them ride the trickiest horses bareback, informing them they would leave the class one of two ways: on a stretcher, or on a flight home. Frustration of all kinds was pushing him to the limit. He knew this, but didn't let up. Lizzie didn't falter, but she flashed him several furious glances. She knew he was punishing them; she just didn't know why.

'That's it,' he said at the end of the class, making a closing gesture with his hands. 'I'll pin up the results of my test outside the tack room. You know the drill.'

They all knew that some of them would be leaving today, and his students were subdued as they left the

indoor training ring to go and rub down their horses.
Lizzie had dismounted, and having put a head collar on
her pony, she was leading him with her other arm around
her friend Danny, who was repeating the course, and who
today seemed to have gone backwards in training, having fallen off several times. Not his problem. He had a
report to write.

He didn't see Lizzie again until that evening when she
knocked on his office door. He was in a better mood. Having put his students through the wringer, he had found his
personal training to be rigorous, but productive, and he
had thrashed his opponents on the pitch ten goals to six.
His injured horse was well on the way to recovery, and
the beer he was currently enjoying was ice cold. Sitting
back in his favourite chair with his booted feet crossed, he
was more than happy to receive a visit from Lizzie Fane.
Until he heard what she had to say, though it began well
enough, with Lizzie in the role of supplicant.

'May I speak to you for a moment, please?' she asked
politely, shutting the door behind her with her usual care.

He wondered for a moment if Lizzie ever broke out of
her shell these days. She had done when she was younger,
when she used to ride like a demon round the grounds of
Rottingdean, but perhaps life had knocked that exuberance
out of her, because all he could feel from her now was tension. He was instantly alert.

'Do you have a problem?' Everyone would have read the
test results by now, and he knew Lizzie wouldn't like them.

'Yes, I've got a problem.'

'So…?' Spreading his arms wide, he encouraged her
to begin.

'It's not me that's got the problem,' she began.

'Let me guess—this is about Danny.'

'Yes, it is,' she agreed.

'There's no one on that list you should be worrying about, except yourself. You're here on your own behalf, not to run a nannying service.'

He stared at her keenly. Lizzie had more than a little of her grandmother's steel in her, but there was more to this than a plea for a fellow student, he suspected.

'I've already given Danny a second chance. She's repeating the course. Last year she had an excuse. This year? Better I get rid of her now than dash her hopes last minute. You need to let this go, Lizzie. And now I have work to do—'

'I thought you were someone special,' she said as he turned away. 'I thought you gave people a chance, because you had been given a chance by Eduardo—'

'That would be one chance,' he snapped in reply, incredulous that she would argue back, and furious she would bring his mentor into this. 'No one handed me my life on a plate. And in spite of what you think of me, I do know how hard it is—'

'How hard you make it,' she countered.

He shrugged. 'So not everyone's going to make the grade. That's something you need to accept, especially if you intend to make a success of a business one day.'

'I will make a success of my business, but this is different,' she insisted. 'This is unjust. All I'm asking is that you reinstate Danny. It will destroy her if you send her away. And she can only improve. She'd not done anything terrible—'

'Or anything notable, either,' he pointed out, determined to ignore Lizzie's plea. 'Am I supposed to wait around indefinitely in the hope that one day Danny will improve?'

'She's heartbroken that you're letting her go.'

'And I'm a businessman who can't afford to have one substandard student graduate from my training course.'

'Danny isn't substandard,' Lizzie argued hotly. 'She lost her confidence last year, and that's all.'

'So, how long is it going to take her to find the confidence she's lost? She's had a year to find it.'

'If you let her stay, she'll prove herself to you. I'll vouch for her. All I'm asking is just one more chance.'

'No,' he said flatly.

'So that cosy little nugget in your brochure about wanting to give people the same chance you had is just a cynical piece of self-serving rubbish, put there to make you look good?'

He stared at her in amazement. So little Lizzie Fane had teeth after all. 'Have you quite finished?' he said evenly, hiding his approval of her stand.

'Not by a long chalk,' she assured him, blazing into glorious flame. 'You don't just have a chip on your shoulder, you have a rock.'

'And you have said more than enough, don't you think?' He paused. 'What's your real problem, Lizzie?'

'I don't know what you mean.'

'I think you do. So, either you tell me what's eating you, or you go back to your room and calm down.'

'Will you let Danny come back? Please.' Lizzie's tone softened. 'She'll be fine. Danny's got as much talent as anyone else. It's just that you intimidate everyone.'

'Except you, it seems,' he observed dryly.

'I've known you for a long time, Chico.'

'You knew me once,' he corrected her.

'Could we put that right?' Her gaze flickered as she stared at him.

'Maybe,' he said thoughtfully. 'That all depends…'

CHAPTER FIVE

'THAT ALL DEPENDS on what?' she queried, her gaze steady on Chico's.

A few potent seconds ticked by, and then he growled. 'On this—'

She had not expected Chico to move so fast, or to reach for her and drag her into his arms. Nor had she expected this to inflame her senses to such an extent that it blotted out everything, especially the past, leaving only the piercing reality of now.

There was nothing tender about Chico's kiss. It was an explosion of passion that rammed her back against the wall as he ground his body into hers. She responded with matching fire. She couldn't have held back if she had wanted to. Chico had unleashed something in her that demanded immediate release, and it was exciting that he was so familiar, and yet a stranger to her. She hardly recognised the passionate woman kissing him back as herself. She had never behaved like this. She had never responded with such instant lust to a man, but this honed and harder Chico was so much darker than the youth she had idolised, and his kisses mirrored this. Brutal and bone melting, they were so very, very dangerous, and she was quickly lost to the point that she staggered when he let her go.

It was a relief when he released her, she told herself

firmly. What if he hadn't? She wouldn't have trusted herself to break away first.

She was not so glad that Chico was staring down at her now with an expression in his eyes that could only be described as the conquering hero viewing his conquest. Nothing could have made her recover faster.

She wouldn't be making that mistake again.

'What shall I tell Danny?' she asked coolly.

'Tell her you bought her one last chance.'

The next few weeks passed in a blur of activity. The weather was cooling down and it was chilly in the mornings. Brazil was such a big country, it was located in the Southern, Western, and even the Northern Hemisphere, Lizzie had learned, but it would be cold in Scotland, of that much she was sure. Cold, like Chico's heart, she reflected on her way to class. His kisses were smouldering, but the look in his eyes when he'd let her go that time in his office had chilled her.

Trying to put personal thoughts out of her mind wasn't easy when she joined the rest of the grooms as they gathered round Chico on horseback. He was such a mesmerising presence, he held everyone's attention, especially hers. She found herself touching her lips, and had to pull her hand away, but it was too late to blank that stormy encounter in his office.

'I have something to say to you all,' he announced.

The students craned forward. All they craved was a word of praise, or a glimmer of approval from the infamous hard man of polo. She had learned to watch his eyes, Lizzie realised as Chico waited for his students to settle. Those eyes could turn cold in an instant if something displeased him, or hot, as she knew only too well.

She kept her horse a little way back from the others,

wanting to put as much distance as she could between herself and Chico. Even when she was concentrating fiercely on her training, she was always aware of him, watching her, judging her—thinking who knew what about her? She could never shut him out. That did have one good result in that it made her doubly determined to excel. She would never give Chico a chance to criticise her work, and she maintained a consistently cool professional front—which wasn't easy when she couldn't drag her gaze away from his mouth as he spoke, or from his powerful hands as he gestured. When he sweet-talked a pony in that husky, faintly accented voice, she was lost, and each time he rode around the ring to demonstrate a particular technique, she was transfixed. Watching Chico in the saddle was like watching sex with clothes on. There was just too much thrusting going on with those lean, powerful hips—

'Do I have your attention today, Ms Fane?'

'Absolutely, Senhor Fernandez,' she confirmed, infuriated to feel her cheeks heating up beneath Chico's unwavering stare.

'Come closer, Lizzie.' His voice was soft for the sake of the highly strung ponies. 'I shouldn't have to raise my voice to attract your attention,' he reprimanded her at the same low volume, his stern tone setting up all sorts of unwanted attention in her body. 'You know how sensitive these ponies are to the tone of our voice, and to the volume at which we speak.'

What were those dark eyes trying to tell her? It didn't help that everyone was staring at her as she edged her horse forward. Chico had relaxed in the saddle and had allowed his reins to hang loose. He was so much in command in the saddle it was ridiculous. And what was even more ridiculous was imagining those powerful thighs controlling her in the same effortless way—

'I've got a reward for you,' he murmured, meeting her wary gaze with an amused stare. And just when she was transfixed and responding in entirely the wrong way to a simple statement, he turned to address the rest of the class. 'You have all worked very hard, and deserve a reward.' His mouth had curved in the way that could always send shivers of anticipation streaking down her spine. 'There will be a guest polo match—a friendly between you and the professional players. The players will of course be appropriately handicapped—'

'They'll be on foot?' one of the male trainees suggested, making everyone laugh.

Everyone laughed except Chico.

'And there will be a party to follow the match,' he continued, 'when you can all let your hair down.'

'That is for those of us who survive the match, I presume?' Lizzie suggested mildly.

The look Chico gave her sent heat rushing through her. 'Survival is mandatory, Ms Fane. The names are up in the usual place for the grooms' team,' he said to the group. 'You'll find the name of your captain at the top of that list. I will be captaining the players' team to ensure fair play all round—'

As a groan went up Lizzie asked, 'How is this fair when we won't stand a chance?'

'Goodnight, everyone,' Chico said pleasantly, ignoring her, and, without any obvious effort or movement at all, he wheeled his horse around and cantered out of the ring.

Lizzie refused to hurry like the other students who couldn't wait to read the list.

'Come on,' Danny urged as she hung over the open half-door of the stall where Lizzie was currently making a huge deal out of picking out her pony's already immaculate hooves. 'Aren't you interested in who's been chosen to play? Or who's been chosen to be our team captain?'

'If Chico's playing, that's enough for me.' She straightened up. 'It's hardly an even playing field when the trainees are going up against internationals.'

'I thought you had more guts than that, Lizzie Fane. What happened to your native cunning? Or is this a sulk because Chico hasn't taught you *absolutely everything* he knows?' Danny suggested mischievously.

'I don't know what you're talking about. And I certainly don't want Chico to teach me anything, apart from equine craft.'

'Liar.'

Ignoring this, Lizzie focused on the match. 'I suppose, if we put our heads together we could come up with some useful tactics…'

'Then, what are we waiting for?' Danny pressed.

'We have to have a game plan,' Lizzie murmured thoughtfully.

'Like we drug the players and hobble their horses,' Danny suggested. And when Lizzie huffed a laugh, she added, 'Before we get ourselves trounced on the field of battle, are you going to come with me to read that list, or not?'

'Lizzie Fane, captain of the grooms' team,' Danny read out. 'And I'm on the team too.'

Lizzie was stunned by her appointment as captain, but not so surprised about Danny. 'Of course you are,' Lizzie assured her friend. 'You're a great rider.'

'When our taskmaster isn't looking at me. I swear, that man only has to glance my way for me to fall off my horse.'

'So long as you don't fall at his feet.'

'You like him, don't you?'

'Chico?' Lizzie shrugged. 'No. Not interested.'

Danny hummed in disbelief. 'Well, whatever you think about him, our game would be a complete shambles without you. Tactics are where you excel, so we need you to put structure into the game—though speaking personally, I'll be happy just to survive.'

Lizzie shook her head decisively. 'Survival isn't enough for me. I won't be satisfied unless we win.'

'And how are we going to do that? Drug the players, hobble the horses, and cancel the match?'

'Confidence. I'll work something out. And, in the meantime,' Lizzie added as she scanned the list, 'have you seen who else is playing against us?'

'Let me guess.' Danny's cheeks pinked up. 'Tiago?'

Lizzie confirmed this. 'And someone called Lucas, alongside Gabe Ortoya, the Brazilian team captain, who just happens to be world champion at the moment.'

'Great,' Danny murmured. 'Shall we give up now?'

'No,' Lizzie said thoughtfully. 'Let's call our first team meeting.'

The internationals rode bareback. Chico rode facing backwards at one point, until Lizzie had a word at the end of the chukka. How dared he patronise her, or her players? They could thrash him without the need for circus tricks on his part.

'So you've found your voice at last, Senhorita Fane?'

Ignoring the shiver of arousal that streaked through her at the sight of Chico in full Gaucho polo rig, which meant he was wearing leather chaps over jeans worn thin in all the wrong places—or right, if she cared to look— along with a top that moulded his pumped-up muscles to perfection, she lifted her chin to give back as good as she got. 'This isn't a class, and I'm not your student on the field of play, Senhor Fernandez. We're captaining opposing teams, and—' *And I don't know how yet* '—my team is going to thrash yours.'

'So you say, Lizzie,' Chico called after her as she cantered off in her matching ensemble of neatly pressed jeans and clean white polo shirt.

They were completely outplayed, but that was no reason to give up. Lizzie suggested a fair exchange at the end of the next chukka—two professionals in exchange for two from the grooms' team. She sent her guys over to Chico's side, selecting Tiago and the good-natured Gabe Ortoya to play on the side of the grooms. Now they had a game worth the name, and the match went down to the wire. It was five goals each when Lizzie snatched a ball from Chico—or maybe he allowed her to think she had—and she slammed it into the goal.

The competition was relentless, the dirty tricks endless—hooking sticks, riding the opponent off, hacking, stabbing, shouting, swearing—Gaucho polo at its best. This was the hottest sport known to man, Lizzie concluded as she watched Chico at full stretch. She had never felt so alive. A change of ends later, with adrenalin racing through her system, Lizzie passed the ball to Danny, but then for some reason—excitement, probably; catching sight of Chico bearing down on her at speed, certainly—she rashly turned towards the play instead of away from it, and managed to collide with Tiago and Gabe, and as her horse plummeted forward she shot over its head, and would have been trampled had it not been for an arm like an iron band snapping around her waist.

'Acrobatics, Ms Fane?' Chico's hot minty breath brushed her cheek. 'I'm impressed. No harm done,' he confirmed when she looked at the pony.

The pony was probably in better shape than Lizzie,

who was pinned tightly against Chico's hard chest, and badly winded.

'You need a fresh mount and then we'll get on with the game,' he said, showing her no mercy. He practically threw her onto the new pony. 'Your team's honour rests on you, Lizzie.'

That brief, hard blast of contact against Chico's muscular body must have restored her, Lizzie concluded, throwing him a steely glance. He'd saved her life and she would thank him—she just hadn't decided how, yet.

'You are preparing for the party, aren't you?'

Danny had just arrived in their room after the match. Lizzie was lying on the bed with her eyes closed, trying to shut out the adrenalin of the match, and her fierce urge to have sex with Chico. Without looking up, she knew Danny was staring around, hunting for some sign that Lizzie was secretly preparing for the party.

'Don't tell me you're not coming?'

'I'm not coming,' Lizzie stated flatly. She was safer where she was. Sleeping with a man as ruthless as Chico Fernandez could only end badly. And she didn't deserve a party after making such a stupid beginner's mistake. It could have led to her pony being injured.

'So, what are you going to do while we're at the party enjoying ourselves?'

Lizzie threw an arm across her face. 'Nothing, and then I'm going to check on the horses.'

'Chico has hired some outside staff especially to do that, so think again, Cinderella.'

'I have a letter to write to my grandmother.' Lizzie had rung Annie, the housekeeper at Rottingdean, who had reassured her that her grandmother was doing well, and would be up and about in no time—which Lizzie took to be a euphemism for, 'There's nothing you can do here, so make a success of that course.'

'Use email,' Danny insisted, distracting her. 'Just as effective and twice as fast.'

'And half as personal,' Lizzie argued.

'You'll miss out.'

'I don't think so.'

'Okay, I want you to come to the party so we can celebrate together. You're our captain, Lizzie. You can't stay away. And if that doesn't clinch the deal, I haven't had a chance to thank you properly for stopping Chico throwing me out on my ear.'

'You don't need to thank me. You deserve your place here.' Sitting up, Lizzie ruffled her hair. 'You're right. I should be celebrating with the team, not moping around.'

'So, what are you going to wear?'

'I'm going exactly as I am.'

'In jeans?'

Lizzie's answer was to run a hand through her hair. 'Look—I even had my hair done.'

'You could put on some make-up.'

'And look as if I'm trying too hard?' That was not what she wanted Chico to think.

'All right, have it your way,' Danny conceded. 'Lip gloss, maybe?'

'No.'

'Eye shadow, or a spritz of scent?'

Danny got the same answer each time—and though she was fast, Lizzie was faster, and, leaping over the bed, she managed to dodge out of reach as Danny brandished a bottle of scent.

Lizzie looked amazing, and he had to thank Danny for getting her to come down to the party. But it wasn't Danny who held his attention, but Lizzie, who was a real little Miss Prim in her smart jeans, clean shirt and trainers. He'd grown to like the look. It was sexy on Lizzie and made him want a repeat of their heated kiss, and to hell with the past. Her cheeks were flushed, and her eyes were sparkling with laughter as the teams gathered round to tease her about her acrobatic performance on the polo field, and to congratulate her on leading the grooms' team to a draw. She played this down. He liked that too. He liked her, though it suited him to remain aloof for now. They had a lot to talk about before he could relax the way he wanted to with Lizzie. He waited until Tiago put a glass of wine in front of her and then he made his move.

'What are you doing?' Lizzie demanded as he came to stand between Lizzie and the other polo player. 'Tiago was just asking me about opportunities for polo players in the UK.'

'I bet he was.' Turning his back on Tiago, who had angled his chin to shoot him a wry look, he moved Lizzie's glass of wine away.

'What do you think you're doing?' she demanded when he glanced at the bartender and the glass of wine was removed.

'Saving you for the second time today.'

Lizzie's green eyes flashed with affront. 'I thought this was supposed to be a celebration.'

'It is a celebration,' he confirmed. 'So why aren't you drinking champagne?'

A second glance at the bartender ensured that a bottle of his best was brought out from the wine cooler. 'I want to speak to you,' he explained. 'So we're taking this to the ranch house.'

'Oh, are we?' she said, arching a brow.

'Yes,' he returned flatly. 'We are.'

CHAPTER SIX

'You've got some nerve.' Lizzie turned to ask the bartender if he would pour her a fresh glass of wine. 'Controlling everything within your field of vision might be acceptable on the polo pitch, but this is my private time, and I decide what I drink, who I drink it with, and *where* I drink it.'

'So, don't drink my champagne.' He leaned back against the bar. 'Is there something else you'd like to say to me, or have you done venting?'

She looked as if she'd like to say plenty but thought better of it. When she firmed her jaw, he realised he liked her like this. High on adrenalin, Lizzie was wound up like a spring. He hadn't seen her so hot for a fight since she was fifteen. But there was a difference today. She was aroused and couldn't hide it.

'What are you smiling at?' she demanded.

'You.' It had occurred to him that for once in his charmed life, Lizzie could be hot for Tiago and not for him. He was keen to test out his theory. Also keen to feel the signs of Lizzie's arousal pressing into his chest. 'Shall we dance?'

She looked at him with surprise. 'Are you serious?'

'Perfectly,' he murmured, staring straight into her eyes—which were darkening nicely.

She sucked in a sharp breath as he curved a smile. 'No way,' she murmured, holding his stare.

'I think we should.'

'I'm sure you do, Senhor Fernandez. But my answer's still no.'

'But this is a celebration, Ms Fane,' he said, addressing her with the same faintly mocking formality. 'And I believe the captains of the opposing teams should open the dancing.'

'Is that your usual tradition after a game of polo? I imagine you could sell tickets if Nero Caracas were captaining the Assassins, and you danced with Nero.' Also a world-renowned hard man of polo, Nero Caracas was one of Chico's fiercest opponents on the polo field. She'd pay good money to see the two of them dance together.

'Touché, Ms Fane.' A smile touched his sensual mouth. 'But this occasion calls for a new tradition.' Both his voice and his expression had hardened. 'And you owe me.'

'A dance for saving my life?' she suggested, recalling the almost accident on the polo field. She shrugged, conceding, 'I am in your debt.'

'For keeping Danny on,' he reminded her, dismissing his heroics.

'You're glad you kept her on now, aren't you?' Lizzie remarked, smiling her triumph into his eyes.

'Danny rides well,' he conceded, maintaining eye contact.

'That's what competition does for you, *senhor*.'

'Are you ever going to call me Chico again?'

'I doubt it.'

'Surely, you mean, maybe.'

'Do I?' Her eyes were shadowed as she stared at him.

'I would hope so,' he argued, 'but shall we address the problem after the dance?'

'Who said I'm going to dance with you?'

'I did.' Seizing her wrist, he steered Lizzie towards the dance floor. There was only so much patience in his bank.

'I suppose I owe you for making me captain of the team.'

'Do you need to find an excuse to dance with me?' he demanded as he swung her into his arms. 'I hadn't thought of exacting a payment in kind, but now you mention it— And as people seem to find the fact that we're dancing together fascinating, may I suggest you smile?'

Lizzie's lips pressed down as she pretended to consider this. 'I can do pleasant.'

'I'm so relieved,' he mocked as he drew her closer.

As Lizzie's tiny frame and softness yielded to his hard body the sensation was extreme. For Lizzie too, he suspected, feeling her quiver beneath his hands. 'Still smiling, I hope?' he murmured as the music began to play.

'I've got a great big grin on my face,' she assured him.

'Just don't try too hard, or no one will believe you.'

'I'll be sure to achieve an appropriate balance.'

'Be sure you do.'

Their banter was born of pure, unadulterated lust on his part. Lizzie was a little harder to read. She was stiff to begin with, when everything about the sultry South American music called for fluidity, for rhythm and abandonment, and for sex—

'If you hadn't saved me today,' she commented thoughtfully when the first tune ended.

'You wouldn't be here, and I wouldn't have had to dance with you,' he supplied.

'Is my dancing that bad?'

'It is a little prim.'

'I can do wild.'

Just not with him, he gathered.

'But, thank you for today.' She relaxed a little. 'I really mean it.'

'No need to thank me. It could be my turn next match.' He murmured this against her hair for the excuse to inhale her fragrance. 'We all make mistakes. Polo is a dangerous game.'

The expression in Lizzie's eyes suggested nothing could be as dangerous as dancing with him. Good. He planned to keep it that way.

She pulled back at the end of the next number. 'And now I suppose I have to thank you for the dance as well. Looks like I'm going to be for ever in your debt.'

He smiled and shrugged, and pulled her back again. 'This is a party, Lizzie. Relax.'

With you? her eyes asked him.

And then, surprising him, she broke free, and yipped and spun around. Seeing Tiago watching her, he caught her close. Hell, every man at the party was watching her. Lizzie was one of those quiet types who, when they cut loose, could set the place on fire. It worked for him.

Dancing with Chico was the next best thing to sex. And much safer. Sensation without consequences suited her. She could move as she wanted to, and express herself through the dance in ways she would never dream of doing under normal circumstances. Dance allowed her to express her sexuality, which was something she had never done before. Being pressed up hard against Chico was dangerously exciting when every part of him carried an erotic charge. He made moving to music the hottest and most necessary outlet for her energy imaginable. And what really turned her on was that while she had her chance to be wild and abandoned, he was fiercely controlled. Chico kept everything under wraps. She never knew what he was thinking, but just for tonight, exactly as he had suggested, she was going to take her chances and relax into this.

When the music heated up so did she, until they were both at flash point. When Chico stared at her, she stared back. He was a sensualist and a very experienced man. She loved that. His engines were always running at full speed. She loved that too. His control was a delicious reminder of the type of lover he would be, and now the rhythm had grown hot and sinuous, with a sexy and suggestive throbbing beat. Chico was a powerhouse of possibility, utterly confident of her responses, as well he might be, when she was desperately aroused. Dancing was the closest she would ever come to having sex with him, and the only things that mattered tonight were the music and the dancing, and Chico.

Heat pooled between her thighs, and she was reduced to snatching air to satisfy the needs of her racing heart. Chico's touch on her arm and on her back was thrilling. Her hand in his, so small it was enclosed completely, felt safe, felt right. She was his for this dance, and when the music slowed and he shifted position a small cry escaped her throat. It was maybe by accident, but with one powerful thigh he had just brushed the place where she needed him most. The sudden pulse of pleasure made her gasp out loud. He'd heard and shot her a keen look, and now all she could think about was being alone with Chico—naked and at the mercy of those sensitive hands.

Had he noticed her reaction? He must have done, she reasoned. You couldn't dance as closely as they were doing and not register every nuance in your partner's behaviour, but Chico probably took such things for granted. Or he didn't care.

The music encouraged her to progress her fantasy. They fitted so well together, even though Chico was twice her size, and at least twice as hard and muscular, but imagining them together wasn't so hard—him so bronzed and powerful, looming over her, his hands so light, so sensitive. He would control her pleasure in the same effortless way he controlled his wild ponies. Chico was known for the most sensitive hands in the polo world. Her throat tightened at the thought. The band had just segued into another, slower tune, and she knew this was her chance to break away—to thank him for the dance and return to her table. She could queue for a drink at the bar, or try to find Danny. There were endless possibilities that would be safer than staying here.

She rejected each of these choices out of hand. Just for tonight she was going to be free from doubt. Chico was in no hurry to let her go, and wasn't this what she had always dreamed? And when reality far exceeded her wildest dream, wouldn't it be churlish to waste this opportunity?

It was a sin for a man to feel this good. Imagining them both naked, hot skin to skin, Chico's big frame against her small body, made her press a little closer to him—not too much as she didn't want to be too obvious about it. The music called for it, she reassured herself. Chico was so outrageously masculine, what was she supposed to do when every contour of his hard body was rhythmically massaging hers? A frisson of doubt hit when she wondered about his other women. Did he choose to be alone? Did he want to get close to anyone? Were there too many memories in the past he couldn't share?

She had promised herself she wouldn't go there. Where women were concerned, Chico would feed when he was hungry and then move on.

'So, why Fazenda Fernandez, Lizzie?'

She was thrown for a moment. His tone was so matter-of-fact it jolted her straight out of the fantasy, and now she realised that the music had faded to silence and the dance had ended. She should break away, leave his arms, but time seemed suspended—

Time hadn't been suspended for Chico, Lizzie reasoned sensibly. While she had been happily relaxing into an erotic daze, he had been coldly calculating her reasons for coming here.

Lifting her head from where, she now realised with deep embarrassment, it was comfortably nestled on his chest, she stared him in the eyes. 'Why not here? It was an easy decision for me to make. The college I attended awarded a scholarship to your ranch, and so I went for it. With my grandmother's approval,' she added pointedly. 'And since that scholarship is funded by you, I can't think that you would allow anyone to win it that you haven't thoroughly vetted first.'

'I have a team to do that for me.'

Of course he had. And she should have known that. Everything in Chico's world was so much more complicated and sophisticated than the world Lizzie inhabited. You didn't get to achieve what he had without covering all the bases. It was Chico's casual manner tonight that had deceived her, but now she realised that there was nothing laid-back or unplanned in his life, because he couldn't afford to be careless. There was too much at stake in Chico's fast-moving world to risk losing it.

'So, why here?' he repeated. 'There are other scholarships available at the college you attended.'

Of course he'd done his homework. Of course he knew that she could have gone anywhere in the world where horses were bred with skill and care.

'You're the best,' she said honestly. 'You train the best, and I want to be the best. I want to follow in your footsteps.'

'You want to go into competition with me?' He smiled, his tone deceptively relaxed.

'I want to set up in business, yes, but in competition with you?' She laughed. 'I'm a few million short of the start-up capital.'

'You're extremely forthright.'

'I don't know any other way to be.'

Chico appeared to relax, but Lizzie doubted she'd ever seen him looking more dangerous.

'I should warn you that I love competition,' he whispered in her ear when the music started up again.

She shivered involuntarily when his hand found the small of her back, and his fingers spread out to claim her.

'And I love it when you speak your mind. It's vital that I listen to the views of everyone on my team.'

The team with one captain, Lizzie reflected, relieved that Chico couldn't know his whispered words and those wicked hands of his were imparting messages he almost certainly did not intend, and in a language wholly unknown to her before tonight.

'If you ever need more help, Lizzie…'

How to answer that, when Chico's fingertips were only a whisper away from the swell of her buttocks? Could he guess how this dance was affecting her? Was he mocking her, toying with her? Was this all a game? Maybe they were both playing games. She wasn't dancing with Chico because of the scholarship, but because of the sheer animal attraction between them and unfinished business from the past. She longed to know the truth about him—all of it, but Chico was making it as hard as he could for her to remain cool and objective so she could gather the information she needed. His mouth was too close to her ear, his breath too warm on her neck, and their bodies were so close she could feel his heart beating. This wasn't just dangerous; this was a crazy, full-of-risk, exciting possibility.

What was it about music and sex? The rhythm, he decided. Dancing was the perfect prelude to sex. Lizzie's breathing had quickened, and her heart was pounding furiously against his chest. What was in her head? Raw sex was swirling round them, and that couldn't be helping Miss Prim right now. All the other dancers were intent on each other, and, no doubt, the inevitable outcome of the evening for them. How did Lizzie think this would end? With a good night's sleep?

'Don't fight me,' he murmured, his mouth close to her ear. 'Once a day during training sessions, that's okay. Here on the dance floor? No.'

'Stop,' she warned him in a whisper.

'Stop? Of course I'll stop, if you want me to.'

Her answer was to shake her head as if she had given up on trying to reason with him, but she didn't pull away and that brought more of her into contact with him. That brought all of her into contact with him.

'You are a very bad man,' she chastened him—and, unless he was imagining things, seemingly enjoying the fact.

'I'm glad we understand each other at last,' he murmured.

All the times he'd touched her seemed to have accumulated in her memory bank, and that wasn't helping, Lizzie realised as they danced on—or, rather, as they gently rubbed their bodies together until the fire inside her threatened to explode right there on the dance floor with everyone watching. Her head was full of Chico kissing her, and how much she wanted him to kiss her again. The excitement when his powerful body had held her trapped had been enough to make her want more. Just thinking about it had brought her to a state of arousal she'd never experienced before. And she was in no hurry to come down.

'Another dance?'

It took her a moment to realise that Chico was speaking to her. She wanted to reply, but it was hard to concentrate long enough to form the words when streaks of sensation were rippling through every nerve ending in her body and her stash of smart retorts was lost in a mist of softly pulsing pleasure. And whatever she said, she doubted anything would remove that mocking curve from Chico's mouth. He knew his power over her was sex. She hoped he couldn't even begin to guess how badly she wanted him. But, maybe he could. Chico Fernandez was said to have senses second to none.

She gasped as he moved his fingers—only by a fraction, but enough to make her eyes close so she could concentrate on the sensation. Her response to him had to be obvious, but she couldn't stop herself. She didn't want to stop herself. She didn't want anything to get in the way of this feeling, though some sensible part of her said she would have to find an excuse to leave the party, so she'd be safe—from herself. But not yet. She didn't want to leave the party yet.

CHAPTER SEVEN

WHEN THE BAND took a break Chico stood back and let her go. She was free to go. She always had been free to go. It wasn't Chico's way to rule. He coaxed… He trained… He seduced…

How she longed to be seduced.

Everyone applauded the band. This was her moment to leave—

Chico thought so too. Taking hold of her wrist, he led her away from the dance floor. His touch was light—seductively light. They'd danced, and that was it, she told herself sensibly. Chico had done his duty by her. He'd danced with the captain of the opposing team, and now they would part. Good. That was how it should be. That was the sensible thing to do. This was what she wanted, she reasoned as he drew her on. This was safe—

Safe?

Chico was steering her across the yard towards the ranch house, leaving the exuberance of the party behind them. He probably wanted to talk, she reasoned. They had said they would talk. There were so many gaps to fill in. They must be heading for his office.

No. They had walked straight the past the stable block where Chico's business office was located, and were walking on towards the big house. Suddenly this was all very real, and immediate. Did he think they were going to sleep with each other when they had resolved nothing from the past?

'We were going to talk,' she reminded him, hanging back. Chico had no idea that the estate he had loved was crumbling, or that her father was in a home for recovering alcoholics, and that no one even knew where her mother might turn up next. So much had happened over the past twelve years.

One look at Chico's closed face and nerves raced in, making her babble. 'Once I've mastered your training methods, I'll start small—'

'Lizzie.' Dipping his head, Chico stared her in the eyes. 'Now is not the time. And even if it were the right time to talk about this, the first thing you should learn about business is to guard your feelings.'

'If ever I do have feelings, I'll be sure to guard them,' she said, stung.

'And your plans too,' Chico murmured in the same measured tone.

'Like you guarded your plans before leaving Rottingdean without saying a word to anyone?' Her accusation hung in the air between them, ugly, and out there now.

Chico's expression darkened. 'I had to leave.'

'Because of my mother?'

He looked at her as if she were mad. 'Your mother?' His voice was full of all the contempt he could muster. '*Dios!* No! I stayed as far away from Serena as I could.' Which hadn't stopped them falsely accusing him of sleeping with her mother, and worse.

'Why, then?' Years of bewilderment filled her and coloured her voice, and when Chico wouldn't answer she made a sound of scornful resignation and turned to go.

Barely had she taken a step when he seized her arm.

'Take my advice, Lizzie, and let the past stay in the past. And don't play me,' he warned, bringing his face close.

'Don't play you?' she demanded, shaking him off. 'I have no idea what you mean.'

'Really?' He boxed her in again. 'You play hot then cold. What's going on, Lizzie?'

'What's going on is this,' she said coldly. 'You walked out twelve years ago after promising to take me away from that hellhole. You left without a word.'

'I had my reasons.'

'Self-preservation?' she suggested.

'You know nothing about it,' he snarled.

'Clearly.'

Chico towered over her, menacing and as furious as she was. 'Do you mind?' She tried to find a way around him.

'Yes, I mind.'

'I'm going to bed now.'

'Yes,' Chico said as he huffed a derisive laugh. 'Bed is exactly what you need.'

There were so many angry words she longed to say to him, but she bit them back. There was too much to lose.

'I left you in the care of your grandmother,' he called after her as she walked away. 'I did know how hard it was for you—your parents, those endless parties. I allowed myself to be persuaded that your grandmother would keep you safe.'

She stopped walking. 'You were easily persuaded,' Lizzie retorted, still with her back to him. 'And you could have said something to me before you left.'

'If I had stayed to explain it would have cost me my freedom. I was a youth with no money and no influence, and Eduardo and your grandmother gave me no alternative when they decided I must leave.'

She shook her head. 'I thought you understood, Chico,

but you knew nothing about my life, just as you know nothing about it now.'

'As you know nothing about mine,' he fired back.

As the temperature soared between them she whirled around.

Lizzie started to say something—something angry to hit back at Chico; something passionate to express all the hurt she'd felt when she was a teenage girl—but as she speared a glance into his blazing eyes Chico reached out and caught her to him. Holding her breath, she stared up. He wouldn't dare—surely he wouldn't dare—?

His grip tightened and, slowly and deliberately, he brought her inch by reluctant inch to within a whisper of his mouth. And when he brushed her lips with his, she shivered and sighed, because she could do nothing else. He moved closer until his hard body controlled hers. Resting his forearm on the wall above her head, he dipped his head to tease her with almost-kisses until she was helpless with desire. Need collected inside her until, finally, it overwhelmed her. She tried to hold back, but every hungry impulse she had ever experienced seemed to have gathered in one place, and Chico's hard thigh was brushing her—

'No—don't move!' she gasped out in desperation when, sensing her crisis, he made as if to pull away.

With a low laugh, he increased the pressure just enough, and the dam broke inside her. Without any curbs available to her, she convulsed against him, helpless as she called out his name and yielded to pleasure.

The final barrier had come down. He scraped his stubble against Lizzie's neck as she bucked against him, entreating him to hold her even more tightly as she moved helplessly in the grip of a powerful orgasm. He supported her as she broke apart in his arms and felt her legs give way. She had lost her last inhibition, and this new, adult Lizzie was an intriguing mix of vulnerable and hungry. He guessed she would soon want more. She confirmed this, standing on tiptoes to link her hands behind his neck so she could keep him where she wanted him as she lifted her face to kiss him.

A woman who could match him with this type of fire was a revelation to him. He kissed her back, tasting her, and enjoying the sensation of his hard frame mastering her body as he drove his tongue between her lips. Lizzie responded with equal fire as he claimed her, by claiming him, and that turned him on most of all. It was as if she'd bottled up every year they'd spent apart and now those emotions were free, they were pouring out. Making soft sounds of need in her throat, she fought him for more contact, so it was a surprise when he reached for her again and she tensed, pulling away with a shocked, 'Chico— what am I doing?' Putting her hand over her mouth as if that could hide all the signs of her arousal from him, she made a sound of disbelief.

'What's wrong?' He loosened his hold on her. 'What are you feeling guilty about? You've done nothing wrong. You're nothing like your mother,' he murmured, sensing she needed to hear that. 'You're too open with your feelings, for one thing.'

She looked confused, and he guessed for Lizzie everything had been left on ice in the emotional sense on the day he left Scotland. He couldn't blame her when everything had happened in such a rush. One minute he'd been giving Lizzie the friendship bracelet he'd painstakingly woven for her out of horsehair, and the next he was looking back through the car window at the fast-disappearing shadow of Rottingdean House.

'I'm sorry,' she whispered.

He pulled his head back to stare down at her. 'What are you sorry for?'

'I led you on. I let you think—'

'That you want this?'

She stared up at him, and for a good few seconds he was happy to let the tension build, and then, pressing her back, he reached for her with one hand, and, with his thigh holding her legs apart, he held her firmly in place with the other, so she couldn't escape the persuasive action of his fingers.

She looked shocked, but in moments she was falling again, and gasping, 'I need this.'

'I know you do,' he breathed against her mouth, supporting her as she thrust greedily against his hand.

'And now you need something more,' he said as she quietened.

Her eyes agreed with that proposition, entreating him to repeat the treatment. Even through her jeans he could feel how hot she was. He wanted this too—he wanted their lost time back.

Chico took the stairs so fast she could hardly keep up with him. Out of breath, and panting with excitement and effort as she raced up the great staircase with him, she clung on hard to Chico's strong hand, though it was a relief when he stopped on the half-landing and swept her into his arms. He carried her the rest of the way, with the scent of beeswax, fresh flowers and baking contrasting oddly with the hot musk of sex rising from them. Chico had a beautiful home, she registered distractedly. How many years had she spent dreaming about his house and what it would be like?

When he stopped outside a polished mahogany door, she closed her eyes for a moment, like a child waiting for a surprise. She was thrilled to find his bedroom was exactly as she had imagined it: a huge bed dressed with crisp white linen, night-stands on either side—books stacked up on them—and hidden lighting that cast a honeyed glow over a mellow polished oak floor. Several other doors led off the bedroom, no doubt to a bathroom, a dressing room, and possibly a gym. And there were French doors, framed by shutters that led out onto a balcony where the soft strains of music were still faintly audible.

'What is it you want, Lizzie?' Chico murmured as he lowered her to the ground.

'You,' she whispered fiercely. 'I want you.'

They came together like a force of nature. Their kisses fierce—her fingertips biting cruelly into his shoulders. She wanted him naked. She wanted him naked now. She had to feel him flesh to flesh. Fighting free, she seized the edges of his shirt and ripped it apart.

Chico laughed as buttons flew everywhere. 'Wildcat!'

He answered her assault by shredding her flimsy top, and casting it aside, then he freed the catch on her bra and let that drop too.

'Neatly done,' she conceded. The fire of battle was on her. 'But I'm not finished with you yet—' Grabbing the buckle on his belt, she fell back onto the bed laughing as Chico's hands found the waistband of her jeans at exactly the same instant. 'I'm never going to win, am I?'

'Do you want to?'

He had slowed the pace, opening the top button on the fastening of her jeans, and then lowering the zipper with an infuriating lack of speed.

'Lift your hips for me, Lizzie.'

She obeyed instantly, and he eased her jeans down. Beneath the thick layer of denim she was wearing flimsy white lace briefs. Tossing her jeans aside, Chico concentrated on the one place that interested him, and, thrusting a thigh between her legs, he opened her more for him.

'Yes,' she gasped out eagerly, locking eyes to drive him on.

This only made Chico keep her waiting longer. Would nothing bounce him into action? With a fierce growl, she ground herself hard against the heel of his hand, and before he could stop her she lost control again in a violent release.

'You are the greediest woman I ever met.'

'Do you blame me?' There could be no holding her back now. This time when their gazes clashed, Chico would see a fire in hers that matched his own.

Lizzie's eyes were almost completely black as they stared each other down, but there was no depravity in her gaze as there had been in her mother's. There was just a woman, seizing what she wanted out of life, a woman who had waited long enough.

'You're still wearing far too many clothes,' she complained, laughing as she moved like silk beneath his hands.

'What about you?'

While Lizzie panted out her frustration in needy little moans, he thought it only fair to help her. Brushing her hair from her brow as she sighed beneath him, he felt some long-lost flame light inside him. Lizzie had always been able to reach him. He had forgotten that. And he had always liked teasing her. That, he remembered. He held her pinned down beneath him with his mouth a breath away from her lips. He stared into her eyes for the sheer pleasure of seeing them darken until there was only the finest rim of jade green left. And then she closed her eyes, waiting for him as she had waited for twelve long years.

She was quiet for the moment, but he knew she was all fire, hunger, and need. And so small compared to him; he was reminded to be careful. Taking his weight on his forearms so that he only brushed against her, he acknowledged that restraint in this instance was torment for him too. The sound of Lizzie's quickened breathing had aroused him to an uncomfortable extent. And she was right that he was definitely wearing too many clothes. Sitting back on his haunches, he shrugged off the ruined shirt and tossed it aside.

'Still too many clothes,' she murmured, smiling up at him.

Swinging off the bed, he tugged off his jeans, and turned around.

Chico's naked body was a breath-stealing sight. He blotted out everything else. She saw nothing else but him as he came slowly back to her. Resting over her without touching her, he was close enough for her to map every inch of his impressive chest with her fingertips. She raised her face and he kissed her…tenderly, deeply. Kissing him, feeling him, running the palms of her hands lightly down his arms, was self-indulgence on a grand scale. Throwing her head back, she closed her eyes so she could achieve an even deeper level of concentration as she stroked her hands across the wide spread of his shoulders, and down over the flexing muscles of his back.

She knew Chico was watching for her reaction, and guessed that the expression in his dark eyes would be faintly amused. So be it. She didn't care. Use me, take me, any way you want, sang in her mind as he dipped his head to kiss her again, and then deepened the kiss. Their tongues tangled as each of them battled for supremacy. Chico won. The sound of their mutual need fuelled her hunger, and as a fierce heat flared between them Chico pinned her hands above her head, making her cry out with excitement as he rested over her, staring down for what seemed like the longest time, before dipping his head to kiss her mouth, her neck, her breasts—

Could she stand this level of sensation? She had been starved for so long. She had dreamed of this for so long—

'Let go of all your inhibitions,' Chico said softly against her mouth.

'I wasn't aware I had any left.'

He laughed, and then teased her nipples in between his thumb and forefinger until the sensation made her thrash her head about and she found it difficult to breathe, let alone speak. Chico seemed to know her body's responses better than she did. She had never been so free with a man—had never realised it could be this good. It never could be with anyone but Chico. Arcing her back in the hunt for more contact, she was glad her wilful body had taken over from her common sense. Chico didn't help when he started whispering the most outrageous suggestions in both his own language, and in hers.

'Must you have such a sexy voice?' she demanded.

He laughed softly, as his massive shoulders eased in a shrug. 'It's the only voice I've got.'

'And these hands…' Bringing his hand to her lips, she kissed his palm, and then each of his fingertips in turn. 'Just don't speak to me, and please don't touch me, or I can't be accountable for my actions.'

'Good. That means I have to control you,' Chico shifted position, so she was firmly held in his embrace. His soft laughter warmed her, while the sight of his brutally powerful body looming over hers made her fierce with desire for him. Once she took the next step, she would have given Chico her trust completely.

'Why are you smiling?' he asked.

'Because I want this,' she said honestly. 'I want you.'

She had always wanted him. Reaching down, she took

him in her hand, and, and, shocked by the size of him, she closed her eyes so she could absorb his warmth, his length, his girth, and his silky, thrusting strength. He groaned at her first attempt to work him lightly, and it was a thrill to discover she had this power over him. And when she moved down the bed to lap him with her tongue he groaned again.

Chico was so relaxed, and so responsive, he made it easy for her to judge what he liked. He excited her and this excited her, so she grew bolder, until finally she controlled him with her mouth and with her tongue, while she cupped him and nursed him in her hands. He trusted her to do this, and even if it was only for tonight this brought them close again, and she'd missed that closeness. Adding to his pleasure became her only goal. She flicked her tongue up and down his length, and was rewarded by the sight of his thigh muscles tightening. Another groan, another whispered instruction, but from her this time, until finally he took her mouth with one careful and lazy thrust of his hips. She didn't have to wonder if he liked this. Lacing his fingers through her hair, he held her in place as he moved slowly and rhythmically to and fro.

'Enough,' he grated out between gritted teeth before she was ready to stop. 'Or I'll have nothing left for you.'

She pulled her head back to stare up at him. 'Do you seriously expect me to believe that? Maybe we should put that to the test.'

Chico's firm mouth curved wickedly. 'You're not ready for this.'

'Trust me, I am.'

Taking hold of her, he turned her beneath him. She sighed with pleasure as he palmed her breasts, massaging them with such sensitivity, she could only whimper out her need for more. Her nipples responded instantly, thrusting insistently against the warmth of his hands. Chico was the master of seduction and the master of delay, and he laughed when she writhed against him, which only made him torture her some more. He was teasing her as she had teased him. She'd brought him to edge and held him there, and now he was doing the same to her. It didn't matter how much she moved beneath him, writhing and sighing, Chico would only accommodate her needs in his own time, while she was prepared to risk everything for one perfect night.

CHAPTER EIGHT

HE HAD NEVER felt such a drive to take a woman. Wanting Lizzie was a madness that almost wiped out the past. She felt like heaven beneath his hands, and when he kissed her all his doubts fell away. Those doubts would be back in the form of 'why hadn't she answered his letters?', but for now nothing else mattered more than bringing Lizzie more pleasure than she'd ever known. When she raised her hips for him, and stared into his eyes with the same hunger he felt for her, no other thoughts were possible.

'More?' he suggested when she cried out with frustration when he made his touch too light, too fleeting.

'Much more,' she insisted, moving restlessly in the search for more contact and more pressure from his hands. 'Don't you dare tease me again,' she warned him.

'Or...?' He angled his chin to stare down at her with amusement.

'Or I'll never forgive you.'

Her words echoed ominously in his head, reminding him of all that unfinished business. 'We don't want to go back to that, do we?' He forced a smile as he shook the memories off.

'No, we don't,' Lizzie agreed, rattling the doubts in his mind with her innocence and good humour.

Catching her up in his arms, he kissed her again. He

had waited a long time for this. Nothing was going to spoil it.

He would never tire of kissing Lizzie, or tangling his fingers in her copper hair. Bringing her close, he dragged deep on her warm, distinctive scent. She flooded his senses with arousal until nothing else mattered but bringing Lizzie into his dark and sensuous world. He deepened the kiss, mimicking another, more intimate act, and she gasped as he lifted her. Spreading her legs wide, she bound them around his waist, while he supported her with his hands cupping her buttocks. She whimpered and rested her head on his shoulder, but she didn't remain still for long, and, thrusting towards him, she tried to draw him in.

He pulled away, which made her wild with want. 'Now, please now,' she begged him in a voice hoarse with need. Burying her face in his shoulder, she cried out as he nudged against her and gave her a few tantalising strokes.

'Are you torturing me on purpose?' she demanded in a shaking voice.

'Maybe,' he admitted. 'What if I am?'

'Brute,' she exclaimed as he lowered her onto the bed and kept her pinned there.

'Hussy,' he countered as she reached for him to take matters into her own hands.

'You make that sound like the biggest compliment on earth,' she commented, raising one brow with amusement.

'Where you're concerned, it is,' he said. 'And why shouldn't you feel free?'

'For once in my life?' she suggested.

'No more talk, Lizzie. Not tonight.'

It was just as well Chico had put an embargo on conversation, as she resented the time she might waste forming words. She wanted him. It was that simple, and that complicated, Lizzie thought as Chico protected them both. The urge to feel close to him again was stronger than anything—to be held by him, and feel the reassurance of Chico's arms around her; to feel his trust, and to trust in him. Trust was the worst thing of all to lose, she had concluded over the years that had separated them. Doubt and lack of trust were so corrosive.

'Where are you now?' he demanded, jolting her out of these thoughts.

'I'm with you,' she whispered, smiling into his eyes. And Chico was magnificent, a powerhouse of muscle and strength. She was enslaved by the magic he could work with his hands, and drew in a shuddering breath as his fingertips grazed her arm. He really was the master of the innocent touch that promised so much more.

'Whatever I say you must do, you must do,' he proposed.

'You'll be lucky,' she said, smiling into his wicked black eyes.

'Really?' Chico challenged her. 'Shall we put that to the test?'

'Please,' she encouraged.

Her excited cries shivered on the sultry air as Chico drew the tip of his erection slowly down, while holding her firmly in place so she had nothing more to do than accept the pleasure. The sheer size and weight of him forced an exclamation of excited alarm from her lips, and that was all it took to make him stop. 'Don't—'

'Don't stop?' he queried, frowning as he stared down at her. 'You're shivering.'

'With anticipation,' she said as she linked her hands behind his neck. 'I want you,' she whispered, moving to help him.

'Then, I'll take it easy.'

'No need.' She sucked in a breath as Chico found her,

touched her, and did things with his hands that made the world and all its complications go away.

Covering his hand with hers, she encouraged him. Heaven was a steady rhythm, and a man who knew just what to do. It was the most natural thing on earth when she thrust towards him and drew him in, though she inhaled sharply as Chico moved deeper, stretching her beyond what seemed to be possible, but he was so skilful and patient that pleasure soon eclipsed the shock of his invasion. Even so, he waited a moment so she could grab a breath.

'OK?'

'Too good,' she managed.

Turning her face into his chest so he couldn't see the glimmer of tears in her eyes, she rejoiced at finally being where she belonged with Chico. She'd waited so long for this, and it felt so right, even better than she had imagined. 'More,' she whispered, digging her fingers into his shoulders.

Chico buffeted her relentlessly to a steady and dependable rhythm, until she cried out wildly, 'Faster—harder—' The first pleasure waves were building.

'As hard as you want, *bonita*,' Chico promised as she clung to him. 'I love to see you like this.'

Helpless and greedy for more? 'Just don't stop,' she begged, thrusting fiercely in time with him. 'Please—don't ever stop.'

'That's one request I can't refuse,' Chico admitted as he stared down at her.

'Then don't,' she exclaimed, letting go in a noisy and violent release.

She would never be able to get enough of Chico. Her whole body had sprung to ravenous life. The more he made love to her, the more she wanted him. It wasn't until he was soothing her down yet again, and she glanced towards the doors onto the balcony, that she felt the first twinge of unease. The party was still in full swing. She should be down there—not compromising her position by sleeping with her boss.

'I'm not finished yet,' Chico murmured as he followed her glance to the window.

His husky voice called her back to the seductive world only they inhabited, but even when he murmured, 'Ride me,' and the temptation to do just that was like a fire burning inside her, she hesitated as she wondered if their raw lust for sex would ever balance with her emotional needs.

'Problem?' Chico queried.

'No…' She smiled as she surrendered. Chico was doing things with his hands that made all thoughts of reality vanish, and he quickly brought her to release.

'I can't seem to get enough of you,' she admitted when she could catch her breath again.

'Excellent,' Chico growled as he tumbled her beneath him.

Resting her legs on his shoulders, he brought her to the edge of the bed, spread her wide and thrust deep, and for a while she forgot everything else, but when he soothed her down and brushed a distracted kiss against her brow, she sensed the fantasy was over. There was a change in his eyes. Chico was replete. He'd fed and now it was time to move on.

He proved her right, withdrawing carefully and swinging off the bed.

'Where are you going?'

She had tried so hard to keep her voice even and undemanding, but the raw doubt shone through, and in spite of trying so hard not to sound needy that was exactly how she sounded. She couldn't help herself. She felt empty, and inexplicably apprehensive about the future. She'd grown up and learned to feel, but Chico's feelings were still heavily guarded.

He stopped at the bathroom door and turned to look at her with nothing but ordinary warmth on his face. 'I'm going back to the party before they miss me.' He laughed as if he recognised that it was far too late for that, and with a wry smile raked his hair into some semblance of order. 'But I'm still going back.'

'Of course,' she said, flicking her hair back in an attempt to appear equally sophisticated, as if having the most extraordinary sex in the middle of a party was all completely normal and run of the mill for her, too. Chico couldn't have made it clearer that this had just been a pleasant interlude for him, and that this extraordinary event for her was just part of the evening's entertainment for him.

'I'll take a shower,' he said pleasantly. 'You can use the other bathroom. Or wait for me to finish, if you want.'

This was all so cuttingly routine, when she had thought the past few hours life-changing. Chico didn't say anything else. He didn't even trouble to grab a robe. Why would he? This was his house, his bedroom—his rules. Naked and glorious, he headed for the bathroom, grabbing his clothes on the way. Quite suddenly she felt like an intruder in his bedroom.

He was back while she was still giving herself a stiff talking-to, and all her stern resolve to get up and get at it, and just put this behind her, fell away at the sight of him. Dripping water and magnificent with just a towel around his waist, Chico was completely relaxed as he rubbed his hair dry, while she was still trying to work out how to behave in this new role of his temporary bedmate.

'You don't have to come down right away, Lizzie,' he said, turning to her as if sensing her indecision. 'Take your time. You can sleep for a while, if you want to.'

How thoughtful. She almost laughed. Real life was such a cruel spectator of vulnerable moments and now she was painfully conscious of her nakedness and quickly pulled up a sheet to cover herself.

'I shouldn't think anyone will notice who's at the party and who's left by now,' Chico remarked. 'So I wouldn't give it a second thought, if I were you. I'll go down before you, and you follow,' he suggested. 'It will be easier for you that way.'

How considerate, she thought dryly. 'Good idea.'

He gave her a stare, and for a moment she wondered if he'd seen through her to the uncertainty beneath her confident words, but then he relaxed and started tugging on his clothes. Job done, Chico was moving on to his next project, and she was a fool if she thought what had happened between them meant anything more to him than that.

She tried to settle back and then sat up again. She wasn't going to lie here, feeling sorry for herself. And she wasn't going to hide away as if she'd done something wrong. They were consenting adults, consenting, and it had been fun.

It had been a lot more than fun for Lizzie, but this wasn't the fairy-tale fantasy of her teenage years, but the inevitable consequence of two healthy adults taking advantage of some privacy on a hot, sultry night.

So, if that was all it was, why did she hurt like hell?

Leaping out of bed, she grabbed her clothes. She didn't need to hold them in front of her as any sort of shield as Chico didn't even look at her. Reaching for his boots, he stepped into them. He still hadn't fastened his jeans and his hard, ripped torso was still naked. She felt a violent bolt of lust and subdued it. That was her body talking. Her mind had more sense. And, for sure, Chico had no such thoughts in his head. The sex had been good, but it was done, and he had other things to be getting on with. Fas-

tening his belt, he shrugged on his shirt, and did up what
few buttons were left, then shot her a dry look. 'You owe
me a shirt.'

'You owe me a blouse,' she countered, her swift riposte
hiding a heart that was breaking in two. Yes. This had been
every bit the mistake she had anticipated. Did she regret
it? No. And she would hide her feelings from Chico, whatever it took. One perfect night, remember?

'If you see Danny when you go down, will you tell her
I'm okay?'

Chico raised a brow as he opened a drawer and reached
for a clean top. 'If I see her.' He shrugged the top on and
then made for the door without another word.

What did she expect him to say? That was great—we
must do it again some time? She'd walked willingly into
this situation, Lizzie accepted as the door closed behind
Chico. And now she was going to see him every day until
the end of the course, so she would have to live with the
consequences of what she'd done. It was hard to believe
she'd been so strong, so certain when she set out for Brazil, and now she'd thrown her whole future into jeopardy.

*Because she had ignored her mother's warning that
Chico was poison?*

She couldn't believe that. She wouldn't believe anything
bad about Chico, but she'd been so young at the time of
the scandal it was hard to be sure of the facts. She could
remember her grandmother holding her when Lizzie had
needed reassurance after hearing her mother saying terrible things about Chico. Now Lizzie wondered if she had
been meant to overhear her mother's increasingly bitter
condemnation of him, which had been liberally laced with
Serena's obvious dislike of her daughter Lizzie.

There was no reason for Serena to be jealous of her,
Lizzie reflected. Her mother was still a beautiful woman,

while Lizzie would always be a carrot-top and unexceptional, but Lizzie's growing friendship with the young Brazilian groom had been the final nail in the coffin of their relationship back then. *He's trouble, that one,* Serena would say as she followed Chico with her hungry stare.

Her mother's words hung in the air now, tainting everything, and goading Lizzie with the fact that Serena might have been right about Chico caring for nothing and no one, which was one of her regular taunts. Chico's childhood, running wild in the *barrio*, and witnessing his brother being shot dead, must have left him emotionally damaged, and possibly incapable of feeling, though Lizzie's grandmother had insisted this wasn't true, and that Chico was real—authentic. He had no airs and graces that her grandmother could detect. *What you see is what you get with Chico,* she had insisted, *but some people can't deal with that type of honesty, Lizzie.*

Her grandmother's words had washed over her head when she was an impassioned teenager and all she'd cared about was Serena driving her friends away, but for some time she had known that her grandmother was right. She had disowned Lizzie's parents shortly after Eduardo had left Rottingdean House with his young groom. Frustratingly, Lizzie didn't know all the circumstances behind their departure, but, thanks to newspaper reports at the time, she did understand something of the way her parents had been living, and their accusations against Chico, especially as she had become the butt of everyone's humour at school when the salacious details of her parents' scandalous parties had leaked out, and everyone except Danny had mocked her.

'See you down there, Lizzie—'

As Chico closed the door behind him all that old humiliation came flooding back. She allowed it a few ugly seconds to inhabit her, and then she pulled herself together. She wasn't fifteen now. This was very much the present day, and she had a goal and a purpose in being here that went far beyond moping around in Chico's bedroom. She wasn't even going to waste time being angry with herself for putting herself in this position. Grabbing her clothes, she headed for the shower.

Danny was waiting for her when she got back to the party.

'Well?'

Danny was avid for news, but Lizzie's mouth firmed when she glanced at Chico, who was holding court in the middle of a group of polo players and their groupies.

'Come on,' Danny pressed again eagerly.

Turning her back on the group and Chico, Lizzie met her friend's gaze. 'I screwed up.'

'You didn't…?'

'Let's just say, I won't be a notch on our lord and master's bedpost, more of a scratch.'

'So, Chico had an itch?'

'This isn't a joke, Danny.'

'So, you did…'

'Yes.'

'And it was amazing. Don't tell me. I really don't want to know. But you did talk about the past and get that sorted out?'

Danny knew how many questions remained unanswered. At a guess, the whole village of Rottingdean knew about that. 'No. We didn't talk,' Lizzie admitted.

'But you will?'

'I'm not sure,' she said honestly.

Thankfully, Danny knew when to leave things alone. They had been confidantes for ever, or so it seemed to Lizzie, but there were some things she couldn't share, not even with Danny, and Danny respected that. Lizzie doubted she would ever tell anyone that she had made love to Chico Fernandez, while he had had sex with her. That wasn't something you lightly shared around. 'You don't mind if we don't talk about it, do you?'

Danny stared at her for a moment, and then gave her a hug.

CHAPTER NINE

HE HAD NEVER had sex with one of his students. He liked to think he had more sense. Lizzie had scotched that idea. He didn't have any sense where she was concerned, but then he didn't have sex with anyone who blew his mind like Lizzie Fane.

Of all people, Lizzie?

Why not Lizzie? They'd been close when she had been too young to touch, and now that attraction had exploded into something so much more.

So this isn't revenge?

Revenge? He certainly had enough reason to revenge himself on the family that had almost ruined his career before it began. If Eduardo had been a different person, Chico would have been out on his ear. But like him, Eduardo cared nothing for prestige and the influence of the so-called aristocracy, and everything for truth and straight dealing. And he had believed in Chico, taking his word above that of strangers.

And if this were revenge, why Lizzie?

As an angry youth he'd thought any member of the Fane family fair game after what they'd almost cost him. But now the only answer he could come up with was that he cared about Lizzie. He'd been incapable of feeling for so long, this truly was a revelation to him.

Forget the past—he'd just noticed Tiago peeling away from the pack of players. The music had picked up pace, and everyone was dancing. The moon was out, the stars were bright, and the spirit of South America had infected all the party-goers, and Lizzie was talking to Tiago. *Damn!* She was dancing with him! Excusing himself from the group he was talking to, he muscled his way through the crowd and homed in on his target. 'Do you mind if I cut in?'

Tightening his hold on Lizzie, Tiago met Chico's stony gaze with amusement, and it was Lizzie who spoke up. 'Yes, I'd mind,' she said.

Brave words, but her eyes betrayed her. Those eyes were hurt and he knew why. He had treated her like any other savvy woman of his acquaintance, and had forgotten this was Lizzie. He stared levelly at his teammate. 'Tiago?'

Tiago didn't need asking twice.

He caught hold of Lizzie's arm when she went to move away. 'Are you refusing my invitation to dance?'

'Yes,' she said bluntly, attempting to freeze him with a look.

'I know you want to dance with me.'

'Oh, do you?' Her words were angry, and two red patches had appeared on her cheeks. He guessed if he hadn't been her boss and this training course hadn't depended on his endorsement, she would happily tell him where to go.

'One last dance?' he suggested.

'Why?' She tipped her chin to regard him coolly.

'Because we both want to.'

They stared at each other unblinking for a moment. He wanted her, while Lizzie was equally determined not to succumb to his somewhat less than respectable charms again, and was determined to prove it by remaining stiff and unresponsive in his arms. She held him as the dance required, but there was no intimacy in her touch. She was like a block of ice, moving in time to the music, while only paying lip service to the hot South American beat.

'This is like dancing with a nun,' he remarked.

'You think?' she queried. 'That's strange, when I feel as if I'm dancing with an international polo player who's hitting on one of his trainees for the second time in one night.'

'You're not just one of my trainees, Lizzie.'

'Just the most available,' she said, tight-lipped.

'That's not what I meant, and you know it.'

She was keeping as much distance between them as she could. 'What's wrong with you, Lizzie?'

'Are you serious?' she demanded.

'Yeah, I'm serious. Less than an hour ago you were moaning with pleasure in my arms.'

'Everyone makes mistakes.'

'You didn't seem to think it was a mistake at the time.'

'Only because I'm not as sophisticated as you.'

She wasn't sophisticated at all, which was Lizzie's appeal. She was straight down the line, with her heart boldly emblazoned on her sleeve. 'And where are you going now?' He reached for her when she pulled away.

She stared with affront at his hand on her arm. 'For a drink—for a walk—for a rest—for a chat—for just about anything that I can do away from you.'

'Relax, Lizzie.' He frowned, seeing her eyes were glittering with anger. 'We're only dancing.'

'Like we were only having sex up there in your bedroom?' She glanced towards the house. 'Let me go!' she demanded as he tightened his hold on her. 'I suppose you think you can have sex with me and then casually come back to the party as if nothing had happened, because of who you are.'

'What are you talking about?' He could never remember being brought to account like this before.

'First you stop me drinking with Tiago,' she elaborated, 'and now you stop me dancing with him.'

'Because you're with me.'

'Really?' With an incredulous huff, she shook her head. 'What gave you that idea?'

'You, Lizzie. You gave me that idea.'

'Me? You couldn't wait to leave back there.' She glanced up at the house.

'I thought that what happened in my bedroom was by mutual consent. Please forgive me if I was in any way mistaken.'

Chico wasn't mistaken, but she was angry with herself for giving in to him—for even allowing herself to be hurt, because she was still harbouring a romantic daydream, while all Chico wanted was sex.

'Lizzie?'

Decision time, she thought as Chico put his hand on her cheek and made her look at him. She had to decide what was important now: pursuing a pipe dream, or achieving a goal. Gathering herself, she refocused on Chico's face. 'I made a mistake, but I won't repeat it. I just want to graduate and go home with my diploma, and for that I need your help, but—'

'*Dios*, Lizzie, what are you saying?' Chico's expression was thunderous.

They had stopped dancing, and all the other couples, sensing a drama, were giving them a wide berth. 'If you think for one moment I would penalise you unless you agree to sleep with me, you have not only disappointed me, you have insulted me.'

'Then I apologise. That was not my intention.'

'Perhaps you need to think more carefully before you say these things.'

'What am I supposed to think when you can switch off your feelings so easily?'

'Says the woman who makes passionate love with me, and who then takes to the dance floor with my friend.'

'It wasn't like that.'

'You didn't dance with Tiago?'

'Yes, but that was because—'

'Because you wanted to show me how I must fall into line?' Chico suggested. 'I don't do falling into line, Lizzie. You either accept me as I am, or—'

'Or I stick around until you select your next victim from the available pool?'

A muscle flexed in Chico's jaw, but to his credit he remained silent, but nothing could hold back all the years of pent-up longing and hurt inside Lizzie now.

'And when you've had sex with them, you cast them off, while they look at you adoringly, thinking how lucky they were to have come to the notice of *the* Chico Fernandez for all of ten seconds—'

'I've noticed you for a lot longer than that, Lizzie. And we both know that this is the hurt of a fifteen-year-old girl talking, not the woman I made love to.'

'You didn't make love to me,' she flared, getting it straight in her head. 'You had sex with me.'

'I think I know what happened.'

'Then know this: I'm not a victim, and I won't be pushed around. Nor am I one of those sophisticated women who knows the score.'

'No,' Chico agreed calmly. 'You're my childhood friend.'

'I used to think I was your friend—'

'And now you're a complex woman I'm getting to know all over again.'

'Maybe that's true,' Lizzie agreed as she shook Chico's hand from her arm. 'But you've changed so much I don't know you. You're closed off. You show your feelings to no one, not even to me.'

'That's hardly surprising as it's twelve years since we last met.'

'Yes. Twelve long years,' she agreed. 'I was a child then, and I'm a woman now—who isn't so easily impressed. I've let go of the past, Chico, but can you?'

'You've let go of the past?' Chico demanded with a harsh laugh as he brought her close. 'Do you remember how your parents made you feel? How they neglected you—ignored you, put you last? Have you really forgotten that, Lizzie?'

As he spoke the music segued into a sizzling Argentine tango in honour of Nero Caracas, one of Chico's closest friends, and before she knew it their heated discussion had somehow moved seamlessly into the fiery dance.

He already knew Lizzie could dance like a dream when she wanted to, and moving to music was in his blood, but this second time around, after hot sex and hotter tempers, was electric. Their dancing was more heated, tense and fierce. If he'd been aware of her before sex, he was hyper-aware of her now. Lizzie's fire insisted she respond to the music, and though she made as if she could resist him she anticipated his every move, just as she had in his bed. Her version of the heated Latin American dance might not be strictly authentic, but she brought something distinctly Lizzie to the dance that reminded him of what that lush body could do. She brought more sex per step to all the required precision and intensity to the dance than was safe and decent, forcing him to tell himself sternly that he couldn't have her at his own party in the shadows in full sight of the dance floor. Thankfully, the tune came to an end, and so did Lizzie's performance. It was almost a relief when she reverted to being safely buttoned up.

'Will you please let me go?' she demanded as if she had come round to discover she had been carelessly uninhibited on the dance floor, and now she was keen to restore some balance.

'No, I won't let you go,' he said, dragging her close, reminding them both of how it had felt to be bound every inch of them skin to skin. He'd noticed Tiago circling the fringes of the crowd, and knew the signs. Tiago was hunting. 'It's not safe for me to let you go,' he explained when Lizzie flashed him a look. 'Wolves are prowling.'

'And you're seriously suggesting that I'm safer with you?' she exclaimed incredulously.

'I'm saying—you're staying here, with me.'

Neither of them blinked as the band started up again, until, lifting his hands, he let her go. He'd felt her body yielding when he'd held her, and, as he could have predicted, Lizzie wasn't going anywhere. Wound up like a spring, she had to have the fire of the music and the energy of the dance to stand any hope of releasing her tension.

'I think you take pleasure in tormenting me,' she said angrily as she came back into his arms.

'You only think?' he murmured, his lips slanting in a grin. 'I think you love dancing with me, so why pretend?'

She huffed and raised a brow.

'Some might call dancing with me an opportunity,' he pointed out, tongue in cheek.

'While I would simply call it a risk to my toes.'

'We dance too well together for that,' he said confidently.

'Stop it!' she warned him in an undertone. 'Don't you dare flirt with me.'

'Or...?' Pulling her close, he stared into her eyes, and

then with every inch of them connected, body and mind, coaxed her back into the dance.

'Don't you care that we're being stared at?' she asked him after a couple of circuits of the floor.

'I doubt anyone has any interest in us,' he argued. 'And if they do,' he added, in a whisper in her ear, 'I don't care.'

Only a few months before, and the thought of being close to a member of the Fane family would have been unthinkable for him, but Lizzie Fane was the only woman he wanted in his bed.

When the music stopped, he was irritated to see Lizzie's friend Danny waving imperatively to Lizzie from the edge of the dance floor. 'What does she want?'

'You'll have to excuse me—'

'I will?'

They glared at each other for a moment and then he stood back.

'I'll watch out for wolves,' she said, flashing him one last challenging glance.

If she didn't, he would.

Denied Chico's heat, the enclosing warmth of his arms, and the sheer challenge he presented every time they were together, she felt his loss immediately, but the presentiment of trouble ahead worried her more as she hurried across to join Danny. She had to shake this feeling off. She was in danger of looking for trouble everywhere. She was in the middle of a party, for goodness' sake. What could possibly go wrong?

It didn't matter where she was, Lizzie realised as she made her way out of the crush to where Danny was standing. She felt like that fifteen-year-old girl again, sitting on the stairs listening to her parents fight, and Chico had triggered this uncertainty by reminding her of the past.

She still wasn't sure exactly what part he'd played in the drama, and sometimes she wondered if she would ever find out. She passed Tiago, who was leaning back against the bar and raising his glass to her, and ignored him as she walked on towards Danny. By the look on Danny's face, something was seriously wrong.

'What is it? What's happened?' she pressed urgently.

'I got a call from Scotland, because you were, um, otherwise engaged.'

'And?' The expression in Danny's eyes was alarming her now.

'It was Annie calling me—she needed to speak to you, but your phone was off.'

Not just off, ignored while she was in Chico's bedroom.

'She asked me to be there for you.'

'Annie did? Why?'

'I think your grandmother's taken a turn for the worse.'

'Oh, Danny.' Everything seemed to crumple inside her. Only one thing mattered now, and that was getting back to Scotland as fast as she could.

'There's something else, Lizzie.'

'Something else? What else could there be? Just tell me.' She had started shaking, Lizzie realised.

'The bank has repossessed the Rottingdean estate.'

'What?' Lizzie reached for the edge of the bar to steady herself. 'Why didn't Annie ring me before tonight? My grandmother must have known, and she would have told Annie.'

'Because your grandmother wouldn't let her tell you. Lizzie, come back here—'

Lizzie was already heading away from the party. She had to leave Brazil for Scotland right away.

'Lizzie!'

Danny caught up with her in the stable yard. 'Don't do anything drastic. I wish I hadn't told you now.'

'You couldn't keep this from me. I have to do something. I can't stay here half a world away, leaving Annie to cope with everything.'

'Of course you can't—but just remember we have to graduate, and none of us can afford to miss too much term time.'

Danny was right. Not being awarded her diploma would be a disaster for Rottingdean, and the equine business Lizzie was determined to revive.

There was no Rottingdean.

She would not accept that.

'You won't leave now, will you, Lizzie? Word on the street is you're going to pass out top.'

'That's just not important now,' Lizzie called back.

'Then it should be.' Running after her, Danny stopped dead, blocking Lizzie's way. 'Your grandmother wouldn't expect you to bail from the course. What help will you be to her then? And you are supposed to be captaining this year's student team against the students from a neighbouring *fazenda*. What about us—your teammates?'

Lizzie was thrown for a moment. 'I don't know what you're talking about.'

'Haven't you read the notice in the tack room? Oh, no,' Danny groaned, clutching her head. 'Chico must have put it up before he came to the party, and then you two disappeared.'

Lizzie let go a sharp breath. Danny was right. She didn't want to let her colleagues down. 'Sorry—I wasn't trying to give you the brush-off. I'm just so shocked.'

'Of course you are,' Danny agreed, giving her a hug, 'but rushing back to Scotland won't solve anything. It's too late for you to do anything, according to Annie,' she added with compassion. 'And this isn't a fun match like the game we played against Chico's team. This is a serious game with talent scouts coming to watch how we handle the ponies.'

Which would be a unique opportunity for Lizzie, not just to impress but to spread the word about the Rottingdean she still hoped to save. 'If I catch a flight in the morning, I could be in Scotland the day after.'

'But you'd miss the match and the chance to impress the top scouts and horse breeders,' Danny pointed out sensibly.

Scotland had to come first, or there would be nothing to show anyone.

'This has nothing to do with Chico, does it?' Danny asked as she hesitated.

'No,' Lizzie said too quickly.

'I'm not trying to say this call from Scotland is a convenient excuse for you to leave, but it is an out.' Danny's mouth slanted as she waited for Lizzie to respond.

Only a friend could say that, Lizzie reflected as she examined her motives.

'This has nothing to do with Chico,' she said finally, 'and everything to do with my grandmother and an estate that has been in the Fane family for generations. My parents almost lost it, and my grandmother held it together, and I can't let her down now. It's up to me to step up.'

Danny still looked as if she thought Lizzie was wrong to race back to a grandmother she couldn't save and an estate that was lost, but Lizzie knew she had to try.

CHAPTER TEN

GUILT CHASED LIZZIE all the way to the door of the grooms' accommodation, where she felt a firm hand on her shoulder. 'Chico!' she exclaimed, swinging round. Clutching her chest, she caught her breath. 'You frightened me half to death.'

'What's wrong, Lizzie?'

'What's wrong is, you have to let me go.'

'Not until you tell me why you're so upset. What did Danny tell you?'

Lizzie was trapped between his dangerously familiar frame, and the cold, unyielding door; her emotions went into overdrive. 'Just let me go!'

'Not until you tell me what's wrong.'

Passions soared as they glared at each other. 'My grandmother's ill and the estate has been repossessed,' Lizzie blurted. 'Are you satisfied now?'

'What?' Chico said quietly.

She pulled away. 'Don't try to stop me. I have to go.'

'In the middle of the course?'

'Yes, in the middle of the course. I can't stay here and allow events to unfold without having anything to say about it. I have a responsibility to fulfil, as the last—' she hesitated, hunting for the right words '—as the last responsible person in the Fane family. I have to do something. Can't you see that?'

She looked in vain for some flicker of understanding or compassion in Chico's face, but he remained expressionless. 'So, you're leaving,' he said.

'I have to.'

'I'll miss you.'

Of all the things he might have said, that was the last thing she had expected. 'Will you?'

'Of course. Can't you tell me more?'

She couldn't tell him what was happening at Rottingdean when she wasn't sure herself. It hurt knowing that, however right it felt when she was with Chico, it was never enough to keep them together, and that this time it was almost certainly goodbye. His face gave nothing away, and when he leaned forward, she pressed back. Undeterred, he fisted her hair, drew her head back, and drove his mouth down on hers. For a moment her mind blanked. Chico's kisses were like a drug she could never get enough of, but this felt depressingly like a last goodbye.

'Will you let me help you?' he said again as they broke free.

'I don't know what you can do to help,' she confessed.

'Money can do a lot of things, Lizzie.'

'No.' She shook her head. 'This is something I have to do by myself.'

'It may not be that easy.'

'When is life ever easy?'

'It might be easier if you sometimes allowed people in.'

She looked at him with surprise. 'Meaning?'

'Meaning, I've got people who could look into this for you—while you finish the course,' he said pointedly. 'It's worth bearing in mind that without the accreditation from here your business plan will stand little chance.'

She listened patiently, but she already knew what she had to do; when he'd finished, she killed Chico's idea stone dead. 'Will your people hold my grandmother's hand when she's dying? Will they explain to the tenant farmers that they don't have a home any more? No, Chico. This is something only I can do.'

'Now? In the middle of the night?'

'As soon as I can.' She glanced at the door, eager to start her packing.

'How long will you be gone?'

'As long as it takes.' She didn't even know if she'd be coming back. She couldn't afford the plane fare, and any money she had would have to go to pay legal fees, and even that would be a stretch.

'But you have commitments here.'

She searched Chico's eyes, wondering if he would miss her, or if he was asking purely practical questions, perhaps already thinking about who could take her place on the course, and lead the team at the end-of-year match. 'I couldn't feel worse about leaving.'

'Then, don't leave. You're the captain of the team, Lizzie. You have responsibilities here. You'd be leaving your fellow students in the lurch, and you'll jeopardise your chance of graduating this year.'

A shiver ran through her at what seemed like an implied threat, but maybe she was overreacting. She steadied herself. 'Some things are more important than ambition, and my grandmother's life is one of them.'

Instead of backing off, Chico moved in close, and, planting his fist on the door, he stared into her eyes. 'You do know this is the last thing your grandmother would want you to do, don't you, Lizzie?'

'She needs me. And family always comes first. The

tenants are my extended family, and I care about what happens to them.'

Chico's exasperation broke through. 'You talk to me about family?'

'Yes, I do, and I'm not frightened to bring the subject up. I expect you to understand that what I'm dealing with now is very much in the present.'

Shaking his head, Chico pressed his lips down in disagreement. 'I'll tell you what I do understand. I understand. I understand family and how they can ruin your life. Why can't your parents do something useful for once?'

Lizzie laughed this off. 'I don't think they're going to start now, somehow, do you?'

They both knew the answer to that question, and as Chico swore viciously his anger sliced through her. He had told her something of his hideous childhood in the *barrio* when they'd had their solitary chats in the stable, and then, after suffering all that, he'd been drawn into Lizzie's family's sordid affairs.

'You asked me how my parents affected me, and you're right,' she said. 'As a child I did feel rejected. If it hadn't been for Danny's friendship, I don't know what I'd have done. I hid myself away at home. I didn't trust anyone, and then you came to Rottingdean, and perhaps I sensed a kindred spirit, because you were the first person I really opened up to. But that girl you remember? That's not me. I've changed. My grandmother moved back in, and taught me to trust again, and how to live life on my own terms. I'll never forget what she did for me.'

'What she did for both of us,' Chico said.

A slow breath eased out of her. 'So, you haven't forgotten?'

'How could I forget, when your grandmother and Eduardo saved me? When I heard I'd been accused of assaulting your mother, I was staggered at first, and then I was angry. It was as if I was ten years old again with a gun stuck in my back pocket, eager for revenge. And after the fury I felt impotent, because there was no way I could defend myself against the accusations. I wrote to you, confident that you knew me, and would know those accusations were lies, but you never replied. That's when I learned to close off my feelings.'

'I never got any letters,' she said in a small voice.

'Your mother,' he ground out, full of frustration and anger at what had been lost—trust, friendship, together with Lizzie's peace of mind for so many years. 'She took them. Your mother must have destroyed my letters. She stopped you having them.'

'We don't know that for sure,' Lizzie, always the voice of reason, pointed out quietly.

'She must have done,' he argued fiercely. 'Who else would do that to you?'

Lizzie looked down and thought about this for a moment. 'Does it matter?' she said at last.

'To me? Yes, of course it matters,' he exclaimed with passion. 'I poured my heart and soul into those letters—' He saw Lizzie's lovely face light with indulgence. 'Okay, my teenage heart and soul, but still…'

'You were right to ask me to speak up for you,' she said firmly. 'And of course, I would have done—if I'd known,' she added, looking at him now with compassion, as if she could feel the weight of his frustration at the time that had been lost between them as keenly as he could.

'Why do you always have to be so understanding, Lizzie?'

She smiled a little at his passion. 'Maybe I understand you,' she said.

He had always thought Lizzie's childhood in the big house as deprived as his, until her grandmother had moved back in from the dower house to take over Lizzie's care. To think what her parents had stolen from her—and he wasn't just thinking about his letters now, but Lizzie's innocence, and her freedom to enjoy her childhood and growing up, as every child should. It beat him up inside even now to think how easily she could have become a victim of her parents' depravity. It didn't bear thinking about. Neither of them would ever be able to thank Lizzie's grandmother enough for what she'd done for them.

'If you wait, I'll come with you when you go back to Scotland.'

Lizzie looked at him with surprise. She was right to. Sharing his feelings was new to him, but her grandmother's illness had set him back on his heels.

'I feel a bond with your grandmother,' he explained. 'And gratitude. I believe I owe my success to her, and to Eduardo. Your grandmother taught me how to sift the good people from the bad, and I owe it to her to be there now.'

He could tell that Lizzie's decision was already made.

'How could you leave now?' she said. 'It's almost Christmas, and when we come back in the new year, it's our graduation, which you must attend, and then it's the match. By that time it could be too late. I'm sorry, Chico, but I can't wait for you. I have to go now. Could I please borrow one of the Jeeps?'

He frowned. 'To do what?'

'To drive to the airport.'

'Do you know how far that is?'

'Well, no. I'm not quite sure, but—'

'You'll take my jet,' he said flatly. 'My pilot will fly you directly to Scotland.'

For a moment Lizzie was too stunned to speak. 'Are you sure?'

'Your grandmother did me a favour once, and I have

never forgotten it. You will travel in my jet. How soon can you be ready to leave?'

Chico was making her an incredible offer, Lizzie reflected, and if he hadn't been quite so eager to see her leave, she might have been more gracious with her thanks. 'I can be packed in half an hour,' she said briskly, matching his mood. She brushed off the hurt. She was worried and strained, and overreacting again because of his manner, but she had to be strong now.

'Be ready to leave when I call you,' he said.

'Tonight?'

'Tonight,' Chico confirmed.

Her mouth dried. How quickly things ended. This had echoes of the past. It was just as well she was leaving before she came to care for Chico any more than she already did.

She had to make some calls before she left, Lizzie remembered, hoping they would distract her. She had to tell her father and her mother too that her grandmother was failing, and the house and estate had been repossessed.

The dormitory was deserted. Pacing up and down, she rang the nursing home where her father lived first. It would be late, but there was twenty-four hour cover, so she could leave a message to explain the situation.

'Could you tell him that his mother is seriously ill, and there are problems with the house?'

'Certainly. Your father's well enough to receive the news in the morning,' the helpful nurse confirmed, which was code for sober, Lizzie realised.

As she ended the call, Lizzie's heart was racing with excitement as she contemplated a possible recovery for her father. Maybe her family would reunite around her grandmother, which she knew was her grandmother's dearest wish. Bolstered by this thought, she called her mother in the South of France. She had more luck reaching Serena, who was always up at all hours, though their conversation was shockingly short.

'I thought you should know. Grannie's ill, and it's serious,' she began carefully.

'And?' her mother queried coolly. 'What's that to me?'

And, she was wasting precious time, Lizzie concluded, trying to disregard her mother's callous attitude. That was life, she supposed, glancing around her tidy space in the dormitory, where she had cleared everything away. One moment she was imagining everything would be all right—her parents would reunite around her grandmother, she would be in Chico's arms, and everything was wonderful, and the next the family plans had fallen flat, and Chico had said goodbye to her without a backward glance.

He heard the news before Lizzie. He was in the corral breaking in a new colt when his phone rang. It was Maria calling. Annie, the housekeeper at Rottingdean, had rung her. He listened carefully and then handed care of the pony over to one of the gauchos. He did a quick calculation. Lizzie would still be in the air on her way to Scotland. The timing of her grandmother's death couldn't have been worse for her. Lizzie would arrive too late. Worse, the jackals would gather when she was at her lowest point. Someone should be there for her—

He should be there for her, if only to fight them off. Lizzie's grandmother would expect him to do something for her granddaughter, and, after what that remarkable old lady had done for him, of course he would be there. This had nothing to do with his feelings for Lizzie. This was a moral duty, pure and simple.

He showered and dressed, and then booked a private

jet, which, in the absence of his own jet, was the fastest way for him to get to Scotland. He was concerned about Lizzie, and about the future of a vast estate that had been in the same family for generations. It wouldn't be split up and sold off for a song, if he could help it.

Lizzie was right in that he shouldn't be thinking of leaving the ranch. It was the worst possible time for him, but it couldn't be helped. The past had a way of catching up, he had discovered, and his return to Rottingdean, a place he'd vowed never to go near again, was now inevitable. Leaving Maria in overall charge, he explained to his students that extraordinary circumstances had forced him to leave them briefly. He would be back in the new year in time for their graduation, and in the meantime his top men would take over their training classes. He had no idea what sort of a mess he was going to find in Scotland, so he had given himself plenty of time.

'I'm appointing Danny to be team leader in charge of discipline in Lizzie's place,' he told them, 'so your training will continue uninterrupted.'

Once that was done, he took the Harley to the helipad, and from there he flew to the airport where he would catch the flight to Scotland. He felt purposeful and determined, as he always did when he had everything under control.

Why then did he feel such an overwhelming sense of dread by the time he reached the airport?

Lizzie was on the train to Rottingdean from the airport when she placed the call to her grandmother. When there was no answer, she called the housekeeper's direct line.

Still nothing. Feeling distinctly uneasy, she kept on calling until finally, to her relief, Annie answered. 'Can you tell my grandmother I'm back, and that she has nothing to worry about?'

There was silence on the other end of the phone. Lizzie's stomach clenched with apprehension.

'Lizzie?' Annie was clearly distressed. 'You haven't heard?'

'Heard what?'

'Oh, Lizzie, I'm so sorry to tell you this, but your grandmother passed away peacefully just a few hours ago.'

'She's dead?' The word seemed so bald and cold. Surely she was trapped in a nightmare? But, no. Annie confirmed that Lizzie was only just too late, which made it worse somehow. 'I'll have to try to contact my parents,' she said numbly, speaking on autopilot.

'Yes, I suppose you will have to,' Annie agreed gently, sounding none too pleased at the thought of Lizzie's parents being involved.

It took for ever for Lizzie's mother to answer the phone. Even so, Lizzie tried to break the news gently, believing that no one was ever ready to hear about a death in the family, however distant the people involved thought they had become.

'You're not thinking of coming here after the funeral, are you?' Serena demanded.

Lizzie was so shocked it took her a moment to reply. 'No. Why?'

'Where will you live now?' her mother asked suspiciously.

'At Rottingdean, I suppose.'

'Until the creditors throw you out, I suppose?'

'Well, yes...I suppose so.' Lizzie hadn't thought that far ahead.

'Well, don't think you're coming here to mess up my life. That would be so like you. You always have to spoil everything for me—'

'I'm sorry...' Lizzie was bewildered.

'Do you know how old Paulo is?'

Her mother's latest boyfriend, Lizzie guessed.

'Come on, you must know,' Serena insisted impatiently. 'I've had a lot of coverage in the press. I can't have a daughter as old as you suddenly appearing on the scene. Do you understand what I'm saying to you, Elizabeth?'

Basically, push off, Lizzie thought. 'I'm sorry to have troubled you,' she said.

'I'm sure the old bat's lawyers will let me know if she's left me anything.' And with that, Serena rang off.

Lizzie stared at the phone in her hand, and then, firming her resolve, she placed a second call.

'Lizzie…' Her father's voice was full of sympathy and concern. 'We both knew this was coming, didn't we?'

But that didn't make it any easier, Lizzie thought, though she was glad that her father seemed to be holding together so well.

'Just tell me what you need me to do,' he said, sounding better than she had heard him for a long time.

'Help me to arrange the funeral?' she suggested tentatively.

Her father laughed. 'Why, you'll be much better at that than me, Lizzie. I'll be there to honour the old bird, of course. And then there's the reading of the will. I'll definitely attend that.'

Lizzie realised she hadn't even thought about the will.

'Be sure to let me know when the lawyers are ready to divvy up the spoils,' her father said, sounding much brighter. 'That's if they get in touch with you before me, of course.'

'Why would they do that?'

'Your grandmother was a very awkward and unpredictable woman, so who knows what she intended? Just do as I say, will you, Lizzie?'

'Of course.' Lizzie's blood ran cold. Her father was hoping to inherit whatever might be left after the creditors had picked over the estate, and if he did that his old drinking cronies would be back faster than Lizzie could raise a loan to save what was left. On the way home, she had spent most of the long flight wondering if she could interest the Scottish Legacy Preservation Society in buying and restoring the estate, but now it seemed she was working on a rapidly diminishing timescale.

'And, one more thing, Lizzie,' her father said. 'Don't let that fellow Chico anywhere near the place. He always was a bad lot, and I wouldn't put anything past him. Once he hears your grandmother's dead, he'll be after you. That man has no scruples.'

Chico had no scruples? Yet here was her father, talking about spoils when his mother had only just passed away, and her mother was more interested in her latest boyfriend than the estate she had bled dry. Another call coming through on her phone distracted Lizzie for a moment. Her heart lurched to see it was Chico calling.

'Don't forget that man stole something precious from me—'

She turned her attention back to her father on the phone. 'Do you mean the horses?' she said, confused.

'No. I mean your mother. Chico Fernandez stole your mother from me.'

Firming her lips, Lizzie shook her head in blank denial of this, but before she heard the details of the truth from Chico's lips she doubted she would ever be totally certain of anything, and with Chico in Brazil and Lizzie in Scotland, there was no way that was ever going to happen now.

CHAPTER ELEVEN

SHE COULD SEE why people might believe that something had happened between Chico and Serena all those years ago. The pieces of the jigsaw could so easily be moulded to fit. A beautiful and bored young socialite with too much time on her hands tied to an unwanted child and a much older husband. Add a devastatingly attractive South American groom, and watch the sparks fly. Lizzie knew she shouldn't listen to her father's heavily biased views, but he had caught her at a particularly vulnerable time.

When she got off the train in Rottingdean village, Lizzie's first stop was the lodge, to collect the keys to the big house. Chico had called a second time, but she still hadn't taken his call. She couldn't face talking to him. Today was all about her grandmother. Anything else would have to wait.

'Lizzie! You're back! Come in!'

Hamish, the gamekeeper, Annie's husband, flung the door wide in welcome, instantly enveloping Lizzie in the familiar warmth of the cottage. Escaping the bitter chill of a winter's day was like a hug, she thought as she stepped inside. There was a log fire burning lustily in the hearth, and warm woollen plaids draped invitingly over well-worn leather sofas, while the scent of freshly baked scones reminded Lizzie she hadn't eaten in a while, but it was the warmth and concern on the faces of her two friends that drew her like a magnet into their home.

'It's so good to see you both again,' she exclaimed, her voice muffled in Annie's enthusiastic embrace.

'Won't you have a cup of tea with us, at least?' Annie said, standing back, having sensed Lizzie's tension.

Afraid of breaking down, Lizzie shook her head. 'That's very kind of you, but there's so much to do, and I want to get back to the big house and open it all up again.'

'Your grandmother's death was a great sadness to all of us,' Hamish said quietly.

He asked nothing of what the future would hold for him and Annie, Lizzie noticed as Hamish the gamekeeper handed her the keys. She didn't know what she could do for them yet, but in spite of her grief she was determined to try. She clutched the keys in her hand until they bit into her palm. These weren't just keys, they were a way of life. The future of everyone in the village was biting into her hand, reminding her of what she had to fight for.

'I'm back for good,' she said. 'And somehow I'm going to straighten this mess out.'

'We're more worried about you, Lizzie,' Hamish assured her in his soft Highland burr. 'So please don't be too proud to ask for help.'

'I won't be.'

But she could use a miracle, Lizzie reflected as she walked home briskly, collar up, head down against the icy wind. She might be determined to save the estate, but she still had to work out how to do it, and with no money and no prospect of a job, and not even the qualifications she had been relying on, she had hardly made the best of starts. She glanced at her phone. Chico hadn't rung again. He had probably given up by now. He must have heard the news about her grandmother's death, and would have rung to offer his condolences. She was grateful to him for that, but he belonged to a phase of her life that was over now. Like her grandmother she would have to stand on her own from now on.

No wonder he'd had a bad feeling. There was a flight delay. Weather conditions were working against him. He was seething with impatience and there was nothing he could do about it. The one thing he couldn't control was the weather.

One day turned into two, with no sign of the unusually bad storm abating. He had too much time on his hands, and started asking himself why he hadn't been more open with Lizzie. Why couldn't he have talked to her when she was standing in front of him? Why did he have to wait until now to feel this fierce urge to set things straight between them? Why wouldn't she pick up his calls?

Passions ran too high when they were together, he concluded, deciding he must kill the anger, keep the sex, and develop the bond between them.

Chico Fernandez counselling himself? What was his life coming to?

Lizzie.

Lizzie was all he could think about. He was worried about her. She'd lost her grandmother and her well-being concerned him. She would be in that big house all alone. That couldn't be right. He tried telling himself that he would be equally concerned about any student on his course in Lizzie's position, but that couldn't explain his seething frustration, when Lizzie refusing to take his calls seemed like a throwback to the past when she hadn't answered his letters. Now he knew she hadn't received them, so were her parents back and giving her a hard time in Scotland? He had to find out. She would be in shock following the death of her grandmother, and at her most vulnerable.

This was so much worse than she had imagined, Lizzie thought when she switched on the light, though she supposed she should be relieved that the electricity hadn't been turned off. Walking across the tiled hallway, she stood in the centre of the familiar worn rug beneath the familiar dusty chandelier, weighing up her childhood home. When her grandmother had moved back in, the house had resonated with bustle and laughter, but now it was dead and empty. Lizzie had felt safe here, but now it was silent and shrouded in shadow, as if the old house was waiting for someone to appreciate it again. She turned full circle, wondering why she hadn't noticed how shabby it had become. The alchemy of her grandmother's personality had worked its magic, she supposed, and now that was gone. When her grandmother had lived here, it hadn't mattered that the rug was worn and the curtains were threadbare, because Lizzie's grandmother had been a strong woman, larger than life, and she had filled the house with activity and laughter, but now it was just Lizzie and the spiders.

So, she'd do something about it. Putting her bags down, she was on her way to the kitchen when there was a knock on the door that made her jump. Her heart leapt with excitement, and she had to tell herself firmly that even Chico couldn't have flown here as quickly as that. And for goodness' sake, why would he?

It was Annie. Lizzie had never been so pleased to see her grandmother's housekeeper. 'I'm going to remove all the covers and make the house like new again,' she explained as she ushered Annie into the hall. 'I'm going to brave the spiders in the attic, find the decorations, and get ready for Christmas.' They'd have a party, Lizzie decided even as she was saying this. The house hadn't gone yet. They weren't going down like a damp squib. They would go out in a blaze of glory as a tribute to her grandmother.

'A party?' Annie pursed her lips, and at first Lizzie thought the housekeeper might disapprove. Why wouldn't she? It was such a crazy idea when Lizzie had no money to fund a party.

'I think that's an amazing idea,' Annie said at last. 'Your grandmother would definitely approve. Come on, let's get started.' Annie led the way to the utility area to select their weapons of choice.

When they'd finished they sat back in the kitchen, exhausted, with a cup of tea. 'Even if we're evicted, the village will remember the party,' Lizzie said with a smile of satisfaction at a job well done. Everything was gleaming and smelled fresh, but then reality kicked in and she pulled a face. 'It's just a pity I don't have any money to make the party special.'

'Your grandmother was much loved here,' Annie said gently. 'And if there's going to be a miracle at Rottingdean, what better time for it to happen than at Christmas?'

Lizzie sighed ruefully. She wished she could believe in miracles, but for Annie's sake she kept those cynical thoughts to herself.

Her grandmother's funeral was timed so there was a chance to hold a gathering afterwards. Even if they only drank cups of tea and sang songs, it would be something nice to do for her grandmother and those who had loved her, Lizzie thought, biting her lip with concern as she viewed the few coins and low-value bank notes she had tossed out of her change purse onto the bed.

There had been one small miracle, she conceded, turning the horsehair friendship bracelet on her wrist. She'd found it when she'd been foraging in the attic for Christmas decorations. Chico had made it for her. She should throw it away, but as she turned it round and round she remembered that he'd painstakingly woven it for her so she would never forget him. 'As if,' she murmured, huffing a rueful smile.

Shaking her head with regret at the way things had turned out, she slipped the bracelet into the pocket of her jeans, intending to throw it in the bin when she got downstairs. She was halfway down the stairs when she heard a knock at the door.

Her heart soared and plummeted in the same instant. When was she going to realise that Chico was in Brazil, and that he had no intention of travelling to Scotland?

Annie answered the door, and when Annie started giving orders in a confident voice as if she knew their visitors Lizzie took that as her cue to go downstairs.

She was just in time to witness a second miracle as a tall Scots pine was delivered. The ghillies from the estate were busy erecting it in the hall. It touched her to think they had remembered, where her grandmother had always put her Christmas tree. 'We'll hang the lights for you,' one of the ghillies said, beaming smiles at Lizzie as she continued on downstairs.

'And decorations,' Annie reminded them. 'And then I'll give you a nice cup of tea, and a piece of my freshly baked cake—with your permission, Miss Lizzie.'

'Of course.' Lizzie couldn't stop smiling at the thought that she would soon come to believe in miracles at this rate.

Keep that thought, she reflected tensely as someone else knocked at the door.

But it was the local farmer delivering a turkey, a ham, and a tray of eggs.

'I'm afraid I can't pay you,' Lizzie admitted with embarrassment.

'Please don't insult me,' the farmer insisted in a kindly way. 'This is my Christmas gift to you and to everyone who works here.'

'I hope you'll join us here to celebrate my grandmother's life after we say goodbye?'

'We'll never say goodbye to your grandmother while you're here, Miss Lizzie,' he said gruffly, and while Lizzie was still taking this in, Annie remembered something that could turn out to be the biggest miracle of all.

'Did Hamish tell you about the new ponies, Lizzie?'

Lizzie frowned. 'No. What new ponies?'

'Your grandmother called in a favour from a friend of hers who owns a stud. She wanted it to be a surprise for you. Hamish is looking after them in the far field. Well out of the way,' Annie added with a suspiciously innocent look.

'No wonder I haven't seen them,' Lizzie said with a smile. Her mind exploded with possibilities. Maybe Rottingdean could survive after all. The ponies were a last gift from her grandmother, and a lasting gift at that, if she could find some way to keep them.

'Chin up, Miss Lizzie,' the farmer said on his way out of the door.

Her chin was definitely up, Lizzie concluded. How could it not be with such an abundance of miracles?

The generosity of everyone in the village was the best tribute her grandmother could have, Lizzie thought as gifts kept arriving. The baker's boy carried in a tray loaded with more bread and cake than an army could eat, and finally the florist called round with several buckets of flowers. 'Left over from my big Christmas order,' she explained. 'They'll only die if you don't take them.'

'Well, if you're sure?' They looked very fresh to Lizzie.

'I'm sure,' the smiling older woman insisted. 'Your grandmother was a good friend to me.'

And that wasn't the end of it, and one of the most appreciated deliveries was a cartload of logs from the rangers in the forest. 'Shame to let them go to waste,' the head ranger told Lizzie as he supervised the unloading. 'A big place like this takes some heating, I imagine.'

'Yes, it does,' Lizzie confirmed, feeling for the first time that she had the same bond that her grandmother had shared with these good people. If they all pulled together, who knew what they could achieve?

'Your grandmother was much loved,' Annie confirmed. 'She did so many little acts of kindness that people want to repay her now.'

This was borne out by a steady stream of tradespeople who continued on throughout that day, carrying an assortment of produce through to the kitchen.

'It's such a shame that the house might not even be here next year,' Annie commented as they shut the front door on what surely had to be the last delivery.

'Might not be here?' Lizzie exclaimed. 'What do you mean?'

'If the estate has to be sold, there's a rumour that a developer has his eye on it, for a shopping mall and a housing estate.'

'This developer would knock Rottingdean down?' Lizzie exclaimed in horror.

'It seems your grandmother never got round to having the house put on the protected list of historic buildings,' Annie explained. 'Apparently, it just slipped through the net, and then she was ill—and, well, I should have said something.'

'It's no one's fault, Annie,' Lizzie soothed, sensing Annie was becoming agitated. 'But there's nothing to stop me doing something about it now. If some developer thinks he can get away with this, he's going to rue the day. I'll keep him tied up in court until—'*Until what? Until she won the lottery she had never once played?*

Lizzie sighed with frustration, knowing her words were nothing more than empty threats. She didn't have enough money for the bus into town, let alone for lawyers' fees. But she had to do something. She had to give these people who relied on the estate for their living something to look forward to.

'I'm going to fight this, Annie. Everyone's rallying round, so let's not give up just yet.'

'I believe in you, Lizzie,' Annie said firmly. 'I think it's going to be a happy Christmas, after all. Oh—and there's another knock at the door. I wonder who it is this time…'

Lizzie's thoughts were racing. Her heart was thundering too. If only she'd found some sort of closure with Chico maybe she could stop thinking it was him every time.

'Surprise!'

Lizzie gasped with amazement as her father and Serena pushed Annie out of the way as they entered the hall.

He cursed violently as if that could make the plane fly faster. At long last, he was in the air, and with any luck he'd make the funeral. He had to pay his respects. It was a mark of honour, and crucial to him. He'd brought Maria with him. She'd wanted to come once she'd heard his story, saying she felt that she and Lizzie's grandmother were like sisters in arms.

Whatever Lizzie thought of him, her grandmother had meant a lot to him, and with Eduardo dead, and now Lizzie's grandmother passing, it was like the end of an era, and the end of an era meant evaluating everything that had gone before. What mattered now was what happened next, as far as he was concerned, and the only thing he could be certain of was that he and Lizzie had unfinished business to sort out.

Just when everything seemed to be going right! She knew she shouldn't have believed in miracles. There always had to be a counterbalance for anything good, her father had used to say, but Serena and her father in league with each other? Seriously? Only one thing could have united them, and that was the scent of money—which hardly augured well for the future of the estate.

Lizzie wasn't sure of her legal rights when it came to protecting her late grandmother's property, but she felt defensive as her parents strolled around, picking and touching and lifting and showing. It was up to her to protect what was left. To underline her growing concern, she could see the neck of a bottle of her father's favourite type of Scotch peeping out of the pocket of his overcoat.

'Come in,' she said, though her parents were already well and truly in. 'Welcome,' she added faintly.

Her parents ignored her. Serena clearly didn't want to waste time chatting, as she was already taking stock.

'Isn't that a Stubbs?' Serena said as she eyed the gilt-framed painting of a horse. 'And this one? Isn't this a Van Dyck?'

'In the style of,' Lizzie's father said, still without acknowledging Lizzie's presence. 'Even so, it's worth something. We need to get these out of here right away.'

'Now just a minute—' Lizzie hurried across the hall as her father reached up an unsteady hand in an attempt to dislodge the valuable painting from its hook. 'All this is in the hands of the administrator. We can't take anything down. It would be stealing.'

'From ourselves?' Serena flashed, turning on Lizzie

with an imperious stare. 'Don't get in our way,' her mother warned. 'We know what we're doing. And we can do it faster without your interference.'

Lizzie glanced at Annie, whose normally rosy face had turned ashen. Serena had always bullied Annie, but Lizzie was determined to protect the loyal housekeeper from any potential unpleasantness.

'You wouldn't be stealing from yourselves,' she explained patiently, standing in front of Annie like a shield. 'Everything will have to be sold to satisfy the creditors. The administrator will decide if we can take any personal objects, and until that decision is made I think we should leave everything as it is.'

'These are all my personal objects,' her father informed her, gesturing around expansively, staggering as he did so.

'Of course they are, darling,' Serena cooed at Lizzie's father. 'You grew up with them.'

Darling? Serena had definitely put her father up to this.

'And you can stay out of it,' Serena sneered as Lizzie crossed the hall to see what Serena was putting into her pocket. Seeing it was one of the valuable antique paperweights had grandmother had used to collect when times were better, Lizzie pulled it out of her mother's pocket and returned it to the shelf.

Grabbing hold of Lizzie's shoulder, Serena shoved her roughly out of the way. 'No one's going to stop us taking what's rightfully ours,' she exclaimed angrily.

'And that's where you're wrong.'

They all turned to face the door.

CHAPTER TWELVE

'CHICO!' LIZZIE'S BREATH left her lungs in a rush.

'I might have known I'd find you here, Serena…Reginald,' he said quietly.

The menace in his voice made her shiver, so goodness knew how her parents felt, Lizzie thought as Chico unwound the scarf from his neck and shut the door. He didn't need to shout as they did to establish command, because Chico had a quiet strength that didn't call for the posturing of her parents.

'You're getting careless,' he observed, trapping them in his unwavering stare. 'You should have remembered to close the door when you came in, but I imagine you were in too much of a hurry to plunder the house.'

'Get out!' Serena shrieked, cowering behind Lizzie's father, who was swaying alarmingly now.

'I'll leave when I'm ready to leave. But as we're all gathered here in one place I think this is the ideal moment to air some long-held grievances, and pick out the truth from the lies.'

'You're the liar,' Serena flared self-righteously.

'I haven't said a word yet,' Chico pointed out. 'But that's you being true to type, isn't it, Serena? I'm guilty of all charges, regardless of whether I even know about the crime. What was it I was supposed to have done to you, Serena? I think we could all do with reminding about that, don't you?'

'I'm surprised you dare to ask such a question in front of my daughter. Come here, Lizzie. Come to Mummy. I'll protect you.'

'I don't think so,' Lizzie exclaimed, hardly daring to look at Chico in case his feelings didn't match her own. She had no intention of looking to her parents for support. It was too late for that. 'I prefer to make up my mind free of bias, if you don't mind, Serena. As I was little more than a child at the time, and mostly ignored, I'm interested to hear what you all have to say.'

As Serena stripped off her fur coat Chico realised that Lizzie's mother was dressed for seduction in a low-cut dress that skimmed her skinny figure like a second skin. He almost laughed out loud. Never waste an opportunity. That was Serena's motto. Who knew what opportunity the funeral might throw up? she must have thought. He was careful to keep his distance from the woman, though now she'd got used to him being here, Serena had left the shelter of her husband's swaying body to prowl around Chico. She made his hair stand on end—and not in a good way. He thought about tossing her in the lake to cool her ardour, but with all the jewellery she was wearing she'd probably sink.

To his surprise, it was Reginald who spoke first. Drawing himself up, Lord Fane said slowly and with considerable deliberation, 'You don't belong here, boy. This is a time of family grief, and if you had any decency at all you would realise that and leave.'

'So, you're not here to strip the place bare?' Chico enquired mildly.

Serena erupted. 'How dare you?' she flared. Coming to

stand in front of him, she lowered her head like an angry bull. 'You're just an urchin from the slums.'

He almost laughed. He certainly had no answer to Serena's accusation. Firstly, he was hardly an urchin as he towered over everyone in the hall—and though he would never have mentioned it, he could buy and sell Rottingdean ten times over out of his petty cash.

'Isn't it rather vulgar to discuss class at a time like this?' he murmured, fixing Serena in his mocking stare.

'It's never the wrong time to discuss class,' Serena assured him, drawing herself up. 'I see you don't deny the charge?'

'Why should I deny the charge, as you call it, when I'm proud of where I come from? My goal has never been to deny my background, but to build on what I've learned from it, so I can help others in the future.'

'Like you tried to help me?' Serena demanded, her voice turning weepy now she had realised that her bullying tactics wouldn't work on him.

'Since you mention it, yes, I did talk to you to begin with,' he admitted. 'I even sympathised with your so-called plight, until I realised what you were really like, and what you were after.'

'What *I* was after?' Serena demanded haughtily. 'Would you care to explain that?' She glanced at Lizzie, perhaps thinking he wouldn't sink to discussing sex in front of her daughter.

And she was right. Chico's attention was wholly focused on Lizzie now. 'Your mother kept those letters from you, because she felt bitter towards me for not falling for her as she expected me to. I needed you to speak up for me, Lizzie.'

'And I would have done,' she said fiercely, holding his stare for the longest time.

'I never replied, because I never got the letters, because you kept them from me,' she accused her mother.

'I was protecting you, darling,' Serena insisted.

'From this terrible man?' Lizzie gazed at him, with a plea for forgiveness in her eyes.

Her parents, on the other hand, couldn't meet anyone's eyes, he noticed. It was hardly surprising, when they had been well and truly brought to book.

'You were trying to lure me into your vile world, Serena, and when I refused to have anything to do with you, you made false accusations against me.'

As Lizzie's mother drew her head back in a mockery of surprise he thought Serena had lost her way. She should have been on the stage.

'I don't know what you're talking about,' she protested, clutching her chest as if she were about to faint.

'Serena!' Lizzie's father exclaimed. 'There's no point in lying about it now. We just need him out of here, and if an apology is all that's required, then please do it.'

'Please, just do it,' Lizzie added quietly, as if she couldn't wait for this to be over and for her parents to leave.

Her father beamed at her, no doubt thinking Lizzie had returned to the fold, but Chico knew that Lizzie just wanted to have a life free from their deceit.

'Very well, I lied,' Serena exclaimed angrily, as if everyone else in the room were to blame except for her. 'Someone had to answer for all the gossip in the village, and it wasn't going to be me.'

'So I was your scapegoat?' Chico suggested mildly.

'Why not you?' Serena demanded.

'So, to recap,' he said, gazing at Lizzie as he spoke to Serena. 'I never touched you—I never forced myself on you—I never joined in your games?'

'As if I'd have let you,' Serena sneered. 'A boy from the slums? Are you mad?'

'Mad? No,' he assured Lizzie's mother. 'Though you didn't seem to be quite so fussy at the time.'

'You were young and ripe,' she said carelessly.

Even Reginald had the good grace to look shocked.

'I can see now that I had nothing else to offer you but my youth,' he agreed.

'Then, or now,' Serena stated haughtily. 'So, if you don't mind, now that you've got all that out of your system, I'd like you to leave.'

'*You'd* like me to leave?' He glanced at Lizzie, who had gone pale, but who was standing her ground. Learning about the fate of his letters must have been a shock for her, though he guessed that this further proof of her parents' abominable behaviour hadn't helped, and he was keen to redress the balance for her.

'What would you like me to do, Lizzie?'

'I would like my father and Serena to leave,' she said in a surprisingly firm voice. 'If only because I can't leave you unattended,' she explained to Serena and Reginald. 'I can't trust you,' she spelled out when her father uttered a wounded sigh. 'And I need to get everything ready for tomorrow, for the celebration of my grandmother's life.'

Even Reginald couldn't argue with that.

'We'll be back for the reading of the will,' Serena announced on her way out of the door.

He bet they would. He turned with concern to face Lizzie.

'I'll leave you two alone,' the housekeeper said tactfully.

'Sorry—Annie…' Lizzie leapt into life, as if a switch had turned on inside her now her parents had gone. 'I'd like you to meet Chico. You may remember him from years ago when the Brazilian team came to visit. Chico—this is Annie, my grandmother's loyal friend.'

'And yours,' the older woman reminded Lizzie with a tender smile. 'And I do know your face,' the elderly house-keeper confirmed, turning to shake his hand.

'Please don't let us drive you away,' he said, conscious that Annie had remained diplomatically out of the way while the drama had played out.

'I planned to go home now anyway,' she assured him.

'I'm staying at the pub in the village,' he explained as he helped Annie put on her coat. 'I brought my assistant Maria with me from Brazil, and she could probably use some company—if it's not too much trouble for you?'

'Why, of course not,' Annie confirmed. 'She'll be coming to tea at my house. And then I'll come back tomorrow,' she said, glancing at Lizzie.

'Thank you, Annie.'

He was relieved to see Lizzie relax into a smile. She looked exhausted.

'Don't worry. I'll look after her,' he reassured the worried housekeeper.

He waited until the door closed behind Annie, and then asked gently, 'How are you bearing up?'

'Fine.'

Lizzie was so tense, and no wonder. She didn't know what to expect of him. So much had happened in so short a time. She was tense, but who could blame her? When he looked at her, really looked at her, he realised just how much he'd missed her.

'You?' she said.

'I feel a lot better now the truth is out in the open.'

'Chico.' She seemed to shrink as she looked at him, and he hated that her parents could do that to the Lizzie he knew. 'I'm so sorry that all this was going on at Rottingdean when you visited that first time, and I knew so little about it.'

'You were always shut out of everything. Your grandmother told me that. You were fifteen at the time, Lizzie,' he pointed out. 'You couldn't have known all the facts.'

'Then tell me now.'

He looked at her and remembered Lizzie's words about how she'd changed. She was right in that she was no longer the young girl she had been, but Lizzie had always been strong—disillusioned often, bewildered most of the time, thanks to her parents' neglect, but she was always strong. And she was even stronger now, thanks to her grandmother and the passage of time. She could take the truth. She deserved the truth. 'Your parents' parties were debauched affairs with everyone just the right side of legal as far as age was concerned. Your parents arranged what they called "performances", and invited people to attend—for a price.'

'They turned Rottingdean into a brothel?' Lizzie was almost laughing she was so aghast. 'No wonder my grandmother stepped in. Now I know what all the gossip was about—and why they mocked me at school. They must all have known. And it was the not knowing that hurt me the most. I couldn't defend myself if I didn't know the truth. So, thank you,' she said after a long pause. 'Thank you for telling me the truth, Chico. And thank you for believing that I'm strong enough to take it. That means a lot to me. That means more than anything to me.'

They fell silent for a while, and then she said quietly, 'I knew you, Chico, and I should have trusted you. I should have known there had to be a very good reason for you to leave like that. And there certainly was,' she said as he slanted a reassuring smile. 'My parents are just so despicable. I knew they were fools—as soon as I grew up,

I could see that for myself. But what they did to you—'
His heart went out to her when she clutched her head in
absolute despair. 'Why, oh, why did I keep on making allowances for them?'

'You always will make allowances for them,' he said
gently. 'They're your parents, Lizzie. There will always
be that bond.'

'But what about you?' She stared at him with concern.
'I feel I let you down. All those years of misunderstanding
after they spread such evil rumours about you.'

'Don't worry about it. That's all in the past.'

'It is, Chico. Is the past really behind us both now?'

'My shoulders are pretty broad.'

She shook her head as if it would take some time for
her to come to terms with everything she'd learned, but
it was time for him to focus Lizzie's attention on urgent
practicalities. 'You're obviously in a bit of a mess here,
and I'd like to help.'

'We're not in a mess,' she said, looking around. 'We're
getting ready for the annual Christmas party, so admit-
tedly we're a bit untidy at the moment, but it's nothing that
I can't put right.'

'I'm not talking about Christmas decorations explod-
ing out of boxes.'

'What are you talking about, Chico?'

'Pride is great, Lizzie, but it doesn't pay the bills,' he
said bluntly. 'I'm offering to bail you out. Money,' he explained when she looked at him blankly. 'Whatever you
need.'

'Whatever I need?'

'What you need to set Rottingdean back on its feet must
seem like a lot of money to you, but it won't be a problem for me—'

Her eyes turned steely. 'This is my responsibility, Chico.'

'I'm not trying to patronise you. I have a charitable foundation—'

'So I'm a charity now?'

'No. But the estate is in danger of being lost, and I'd like to help so you can keep it in the family. As your grandmother helped me,' he reminded her.

'This is my home, Chico. It's mine to save. I do appreciate your offer of help, but no, thank you.'

'You'd risk throwing people like Annie out on the streets, rather than accept help from me?'

'That's unfair.'

'Is it?'

'And if I accept this offer of yours? What's the catch?'

He looked at her quizzically. 'I don't know what you mean.'

'Chico, there's always a catch. You're not going to write a blank cheque and let me get on with it.'

'Well, no, I'm not,' he admitted, raking his hair, to give himself time to think.

'So?' Lizzie pressed. 'What's the catch?'

'Here's what I'll do. I'll open an account and deposit sufficient funds to take care of all the renovations and to pay off the creditors, and I'll send my best managers in to take charge. And then, obviously, you'll come back with me to Brazil.'

'There's nothing obvious about it,' Lizzie exclaimed. 'At least, not to me.'

'So you don't want to finish the course, play in the match, or be awarded your diploma?'

'I want all those things, but not with any strings attached. If I come back, we both know what will happen, and I don't want to be accused by anyone of sleeping my way to a diploma.'

'That would never happen. You're more than good enough to pass the course without sleeping with the boss.'

'And I don't want you spreading your money around so I'm always in debt to you.'

'You would never be indebted to me. I've already told you—'

'How rich you are?' Lizzie interrupted him. 'Here in Rottingdean we help each other out regardless of how rich or poor we are, and, whether I've got money or not, I'll find some way to help these people. I'm not going to let them down.'

'You don't want to let them down,' he argued, 'but without a large injection of cash you don't stand a chance of saving the estate. And where else are you going to get the money, Lizzie?'

'I'll find a way,' she said stubbornly.

'I would love nothing more than to believe you, but for once you've taken on more than you can handle.'

She braced her shoulders. 'Didn't you say you had a bed in the village?'

'Yes. At the pub,' he confirmed.

She stared pointedly at him, telling him it was time to go.

'I'll bid you goodnight,' he said formally.

'Goodnight, Chico.' Walking to the door, she held it open for him. 'Thank you for being here when I needed you.'

He smiled wryly. 'Somehow I think you could have handled them on your own.'

'Maybe,' Lizzie agreed with a thin smile. 'But I'm glad we got the truth out of them at last.'

'Nothing we didn't already know, or suspect,' he said. 'But, as you say, it was good to get it out in the open, though it must have been a shock for you when they turned up on your doorstep.'

'It was quite a shock,' Lizzie admitted, holding his stare as she rested back against the door, 'but not nearly as much of a surprise as when you made your entrance.'

'Glad I could be of assistance,' he said dryly. 'Goodnight, Lizzie.'

She made a soft little sound when he caught her close on his way out of the door. He brushed her lips with his, and then, because he couldn't resist, he deepened the kiss, and Lizzie tasted every bit as good as he remembered—possibly even better, now they were back together at Rottingdean, where memories pooled and swirled around them.

'So you're leaving me again?' she said when he pulled away.

'I'm not leaving you again,' he argued gently. 'I wouldn't have left the first time, if Eduardo had allowed me to stay. But what could I offer you then, Lizzie? A dream we made up in the stable? I had to go when Eduardo left. I had no money to do as I pleased. But tonight you shouldn't be alone, so I'm going to ask Annie to come back and stay with you.'

He didn't add that the next time he took Lizzie to bed would be at the right time and for all the right reasons, and that wasn't now.

CHAPTER THIRTEEN

SHE WAS A small, slight figure, muffled up against the sharp, icy wind in a black coat that looked several sizes too big for her and a scarf that could have served as a blanket for a medium-sized pony. Her hair was whipping around her face, and she looked pale and strained, but composed. The cemetery was full. So full, people were lining the railings outside, and the surrounding streets were cordoned off to cope with the crowds. The village of Rottingdean and the surrounding area had come to a standstill. All the small shops had closed for the day. There would have been no point opening when everyone was at the funeral. What a wonderful legacy for anyone to leave, he thought as he walked up to the grave.

Lizzie remained rigidly in place as the single red rose landed on the coffin. She didn't turn to see who had dropped it onto the polished mahogany casket. Every sense she possessed gave her the answer to that question. She was glad to have Chico's reassuring presence close by. She had expected the ceremony to be smaller and more private. Discovering her grandmother had done so many kind deeds for people over the years made her loss even harder to bear and the grief keener. Lizzie had hoped she could hide away and contain her sadness, but that had not been possible. The people had decided that her grandmother would be sent off with a skirl of the pipes and a chorus of happy songs from the local school children. And she was proud and happy for her grandmother, if lost and grief-stricken for herself. But none of this could show. She still had an estate to save. As her grandmother would have done, she lifted her chin and stared into a future that was hers to mould. Feeling Chico at her side as the final ceremony drew to a close, she turned to face him and felt the familiar tug of longing as she did so.

'Thank you for coming.'

His concerned gaze was steady on her face. He turned to the older woman at his side. 'You remember Maria?'

'Yes, of course I do.' Lizzie smiled warmly. 'It's very good of you to come all this way.'

'I had to be here.' Maria gave her a hug of the same calibre as Annie's, and if anything could bring tears to Lizzie's eyes, it was that warmth, that genuine affection.

'I'm very sorry for your loss, Lizzie,' Maria said gently, letting go of her hands. 'I'm so glad I could be here to celebrate your grandmother's life with you. Chico tells me she was a remarkable lady.'

'She was,' Lizzie confirmed softly.

'Ah, there's Annie,' Maria said. 'Will you both excuse me? I promised to help at the house when everyone arrives.'

'Of course.'

Now they were alone again, Chico's dark stare reached down into her soul, grabbed it tight and squeezed it hard. She was a lost cause where Chico was concerned, Lizzie concluded ruefully. 'I have to stay and thank everyone,' she explained. 'There's no point in you standing here freezing.'

'And if I want to stand here freezing?'

'Then, I can't stop you, but don't you ever tire of playing the white knight?'

'I can be bad.'

Heat coursed through her. No one knew that better than she did.

Chico remained at her side until she had thanked the last mourner. He was like a brazier of moral warmth: strong, firm, and reassuring. If she closed her mind to all the financial problems she was facing, she could almost believe everything would be all right. She would save the estate—convince the bank to back her, and the heritage society to take on the responsibility of Rottingdean House to protect it from greedy developers—

But, would it? Would it be all right?

She had to put all that out of her mind as the minister of the small village kirk came to offer his support and Chico took that as his cue to leave.

'Won't you come back to the house?'

He turned to look at her and her heart squeezed tight. Wind-whipped and resolute, Chico was so brazenly strong and piratical, his dark eyes and swarthy skin so violently at odds with the fair Celts surrounding him.

'I'll give you a chance to collect yourself, and come by later.'

Her stomach dropped with disappointment. She didn't know when he planned to leave and go back to Brazil, so every moment she could spend with him was infinitely precious now. 'Everyone's heading up to the house,' she called back. 'And Maria's there, helping Anna.'

With a nod of his head, he turned to walk away. Which way would he go? she wondered as Chico paused to speak to those who thought they remembered the dark stranger from some years back. She couldn't help but notice how pleasant he was with everyone, and how people liked him, and then she was swept up in a phalanx of mourners, all heading to the big house for the wake, and she lost sight of him.

It was impossible to carry her worries back to the house when the pipers were leading them forward with a jaunty tune, and she was safe in the middle of a haven of warmth and support, full of the grit and humour that was so typical of Rottingdean. There had been hard times before, and there might be hard times again, but the people of Rottingdean stuck together, and that was how they got through them. Anecdotes about her grandmother made the brisk walk short and pleasant, so that by the time they arrived at the house Lizzie was so bolstered by all the good cheer and support she was receiving, she had almost forgotten the challenges she faced. The first of these was waiting for her outside the front door.

So that was why Chico had rushed back.

He had wanted to surprise her, and had to be back to receive the van and driver, who had parked up at the bottom of the steps. The van doors were open and Lizzie could see hampers of food and cases of her grandmother's favourite pink champagne.

'After all these years, you remembered,' she exclaimed.

'Your grandmother's favourite champagne?' Chico shrugged. 'A great lady deserves a great send-off, and I haven't forgotten a single thing about the days I spent here.'

Lizzie took a second look at the expression in his eyes. Chico Fernandez, the man reputed to care for nothing and no one, except the game of polo, was showing emotion, and plenty of it. The thought that he was capable of feeling showed how much he'd changed, and that was all it took to make her heart thunder.

He was pleased to see Maria enjoying the gathering. She seemed to have formed an immediate friendship with

Annie, and the two women were busy distributing drinks and food. Lizzie was a natural with everyone, but he could see exhaustion building behind her eyes. It had been a long day for her, and she'd had a mountain to climb since returning to Scotland, and there would be more problems ahead. In a few days' time the will would be read, which meant her parents would be back. Vultures never stayed away for long. Meanwhile, lights were blazing, and the old house had come back to life again, thanks to Lizzie. Fires were blazing in the hearths, and there were small gifts for everyone to take home with them, each of them carefully wrapped beneath a beautifully decorated Christmas tree. He had no fears for Lizzie. It was only natural that she was tired now, but she had more of her grandmother in her than she knew.

He stayed at the wake as long as was politely necessary, and then he took up an invitation by the gamekeeper Hamish to look round the estate.

'A breath of fresh air is what we both need, I think,' Hamish told him as he led the way.

'I couldn't agree with you more,' he said, glancing back at Lizzie, who had been studiously ignoring him since he arrived. He hadn't said when he would be leaving, and he guessed she didn't want to make the same mistake she'd made fifteen years ago by thinking he would always be around. As far as Lizzie was concerned, this was day one of her new life, and, like everything else she did, he knew she would stride boldly forward into the future with or without him.

It was a grand old estate, and on the slim funds Hamish had had to play with he'd worked miracles. 'I'm impressed,' Chico admitted, remembering that he had done something very similar himself in Brazil.

'This is a lifetime's work.'

'And you could use some help,' Chico suggested.

'It wouldn't go amiss,' Hamish agreed gruffly as they shook hands. 'Will we be seeing you tomorrow?'

'I expect so.' This was a man with whom he was already forming a firm bond of respect, Chico acknowledged, but he wasn't ready to reveal his plans to anyone yet.

'That's good,' Hamish said, shooting him the straight look he might give to a man in whom Hamish believed he could place his trust.

Biting her lip so it hurt enough to stop her crying when she thought about all the kind words for her grandmother, Lizzie closed the door on the last of their guests. Leaning back with her eyes tightly shut, she closed her heart too. Where was Chico? And why was she wasting even more time caring about a man who was probably on his way back to Brazil by now?

Walking into the library, she opened the desk drawer where Annie had put the letter from the bank. Bringing it out, she read it again to be sure there was no mistake. She had also found a stash of unopened bills in her grandmother's dressing table that had lain untouched since her grandmother had been taken ill. The letter from the bank was quite specific. The last of the ponies and the livestock would go, and then the land would be parcelled up, and the house sold off. Everything Lizzie's grandmother had worked so hard to build up would be torn down and sold off for a fraction of its value. She would have to let the staff go—tell them the estate was going to be sold, and they would have to make other plans. She had a few personal trinkets to sell, and she would share that money between the tenants and staff. It was a derisory amount for generations of loyalty, but it was all she could do for them.

'Am I interrupting?'

'Chico? I thought you'd gone.' She gulped in a breath as her heart went crazy with shock.

'Annie gave me the keys.' He held them up. 'I hope you don't mind. I didn't think you should be alone tonight.'

'I told you before. I'm fine,' she insisted.

'Will you stop saying you're fine, when it's clear to me that you're anything but fine?'

He tossed the keys in a dish by the door and walked towards her, shedding his scarf and jacket along the way. He'd already taken off the tie he'd worn earlier, and his shirt had a few buttons undone at the neck.

'You look tired too,' she said as he came closer.

'Me?' Chico's smile was slow, and now he was standing close enough for her to detect his clean spicy scent, and the chill of the winter air on his face. She was surprised to feel a frisson of awareness pass between them even now when she was at her lowest ebb.

'I think it's time for you to go to bed. It's been a long day for you, Lizzie.'

Surely, he didn't mean with him? She glanced at the door, wondering how to politely broach the subject of him leaving. She couldn't take any false dawns today. It would be the best thing ever to sleep with Chico, and have his comfort throughout the night, but not when morning came and she was alone again.

'Do you want me to carry you upstairs?' he offered, trying to inject a little lightness into her gloomy thoughts.

'No. But thank you.' What irony, when she had never needed the reassurance of Chico's arms more, but if she gave in to this yearning and he returned to Brazil, she would feel doubly deserted.

'But I insist,' he said. Before she could protest, Chico had swept her off her feet and carried her out of the library, and straight upstairs to the bathroom adjoining her bedroom.

'I'm going to run a bath for you,' he said, setting her down on a chair in the corner, 'but first I'm going to wash the tears from your face.'

'Tears?' Her hand flew to her face. Chico gently brought it down again.

He ran the water until it was warm, and then soaked a flannel, wringing it out before wiping her face.

'You don't have to do that.'

'But I want to,' he said, making a thorough job of it. 'You need to let go of everything and just relax now, Lizzie.'

But not too much, she thought, watching as Chico squeezed toothpaste onto her brush. 'You've changed,' she said softly.

'Me? Changed?' His lips pressed down wryly. 'Are you sure?'

'Oh, yes, I'm sure,' she said confidently. 'You can feel again. You can look into my eyes and feel what I feel, and then reach out to me. We used to share things, Chico, but you were always guarded.'

'And now I'm not?'

'No, you're not,' she said with conviction. 'Maybe in business you have to be careful, but you're not careful with me when you express your feelings. Just now when you wiped my face—you're either an amazing actor, or you really care.'

'I really care,' Chico said slowly and deliberately.

'Yes. I believe you do.'

'You take a bath,' he said, straightening up and adopting a matter-of-fact manner. 'I'm going to leave you now, but I'll be within shouting distance, if you need me.'

'There's a bedroom next door.' It was all made up in

case guests had wanted to stay. 'You're quite welcome…'
Her voice tailed away. She had no idea what Chico intended.

'I'll be back,' he promised. 'Take your bath, then get into your nightclothes and I'll tuck you into bed.'

That sounded like heaven, Lizzie thought. Now she was no longer on show, exhaustion was sweeping over her in big, drowning waves.

She bathed, dried herself and got into her pyjamas on autopilot. She was practically asleep by the time she was ready to climb into bed.

'Oh, hello,' she said with surprise, seeing Chico had already made himself comfortable on the opposite side of her bed.

'I hope you don't mind,' he said, shooting her a wry look, 'but in the absence of night attire, I'm wearing my boxers.'

'Mind?' she said vaguely. Why should she mind him wearing boxers? Wasn't the fact that he was in her bed more alarming? Maybe, but she was beat and didn't have the energy to fight him. 'So long as you're not naked,' she mumbled. Even speaking was an effort now.

'I'm not naked, so come here. I want to sleep with you.'

First hurdles first, Lizzie concluded. Could she get into bed without touching him? Her throat dried as she watched Chico's impressive muscles flexing as he shifted position to make room for her on the bed. Hadn't he listened to a single word she'd said? She was tired—exhausted—and badly in need of not being hurt.

'Lizzie…'

As Chico held out his hand she hesitated, and then climbed in, or, more accurately, she sank boneless with exhaustion into the bed at his side. She tensed briefly when

Chico put his arms around her and drew her close, but he felt so good, so safe and warm, and she was so very tired…

'Sleep,' he murmured, stroking the hair back from her brow.

'You really mean it,' she managed groggily as her eyelids grew impossibly heavy. 'You really want to sleep with me.'

'Of course I want to sleep with you. I love you, Lizzie Fane.'

Was that a dream, or had Chico really said that? It was the last thing she remembered until she woke up at dawn.

Was this a dream? If it was a dream, it was the best dream ever. It was a comfortable, sleepy dream that comprised of nothing but sensation. And what sensation…

'Chico,' she whispered, relishing his touch. Brushing against her, he was dealing the most exquisite pleasure… pleasure that should go on and on. She never wanted this to end. Did she have to wake up? 'Am I dreaming?'

'I don't know. Are you dreaming?' Chico murmured, smiling against her mouth.

'Don't talk,' she whispered. 'It distracts me.' She sighed with pleasure as he continued the gentle, rhythmic strokes so carefully placed, and so dependably accurate. 'If this is a dream, please don't wake me up.'

'You'll have to wake up at some point.' As he said this Chico settled deep and did something amazing that made warm sudsy sensation wash over her as the dam broke.

'I think you're awake now,' he observed with amusement when she had finally quietened.

'Can I go to sleep now, and wake up again just like that?'

She opened her eyes reluctantly when Chico didn't answer, to see him smiling down into her face.

'Good morning, Lizzie.'

'That was such a great way to wake up. And, you, braced on your forearms—that's not a bad sight, either. Do we really have to get up now?'

'Unfortunately, yes. I have business today.'

'Business?' She was wide awake instantly. As awake as if she'd stepped under a cold shower.

Will this business take you away for long? she longed to ask him, but Chico had done enough for her, and hadn't she vowed to make her own life? What more did she want from him?

Everything?

CHAPTER FOURTEEN

THE HOUSE FELT so empty now Chico had gone, so she got busy. She had business to attend to.

She grew increasingly anxious as the morning progressed, having drawn a disappointing blank everywhere. Most of the institutions that she had hoped to approach with a view to them bailing out the estate, short-term at least, had already closed for the holidays.

By the morning of the third day, Lizzie was in despair. There was no sign of any movement on the financial front, and, worse, no sign of Chico.

She couldn't allow him to distract her, she determined, firming her resolve, and she would not give up. Rottingdean was a far bigger cause than her own hopes and dreams.

That thought took her through almost to the end of that working day, when, swallowing her pride, she called him.

'Senhor Fernandez is locked in conference with his lawyers and cannot be disturbed.'

'Have you any idea when he'll be free?'

'None, I'm afraid.'

The voice at the other end of the line was cool and impartial. Why should she expect it to be any different?

Just when she thought bad couldn't get any worse, it got worse. Her mother called.

'There's no point in you coming all this way for the reading of the will. It's irrelevant now,' Lizzie tried to explain. 'There's nothing left—not for you, not for me, and, more importantly, not for any of the tenants.'

'Never mind the tenants,' her mother blazed back. 'What about your grandmother's jewellery? She had some valuable pieces. Surely you had enough sense to squirrel some of them away?'

'All gone,' Lizzie intoned, staring at the sparkling diamonds in her hand.

She'd seen the will and had cried when she'd read it. Her grandmother had left her everything, no doubt hoping Lizzie would continue with the work of breeding horses and rebuilding the estate that her grandmother had so bravely and so optimistically begun so late in her long life. The first person Lizzie had contacted was her grandmother's solicitor to check that the will she had in her hand was a true copy of the one he had on file. She also wanted to know if there was any money, any assets, or anything at all that could be sold off to save the estate.

'You can't sell any of the livestock, the pictures, or the silver and ornaments, as they go with the house,' the solicitor said, confirming what Lizzie believed to be the case, 'but any personal effects handed to you by your grandmother as a gift are yours to keep.'

'I have some pieces of jewellery I can sell. I will split the proceeds between the tenants.'

She held the jewellery to her face for a moment, imagining she could smell her grandmother's familiar lavender scent lingering on the sparkling stones. It wasn't the value, but the memories each piece held that she would miss. But practicality demanded that she sell them, Lizzie reminded herself as she packed each item neatly in a box.

There was always a darkest part of the night, Lizzie

reflected as the courier arrived to take her grandmother's jewellery away. She didn't just feel a failure; she was a failure who had to sell her grandmother's precious jewellery. But far worse than that, all her brave words about saving the estate had come to nothing. It was hard to believe the staff had stayed on. They were supposed to have gone by now, as the sale of the house and contents was tomorrow and there was nothing more for them to do. But they were still here, giving Lizzie all their support, which she didn't feel she'd earned. This level of loyalty and kindness in the face of disaster was typical of everyone on the estate.

Even the moon had gone behind a cloud, Lizzie realised ruefully as she stared out of the window in her bedroom. She had one more night in the old house, burning the last of the logs gifted to her, and remembering happier times with her grandmother.

Her parents—not so much, Lizzie accepted wryly as she hunkered down on the window seat to hug her knees. It was vital to keep a sense of humour if she was going to survive the next few days. She stared out over the lake where moonlight was streaming like a silver banner, remembering that tomorrow the last of the horses would go, even the precious colts her grandmother had bred, and next to go would be all the contents in the house, until finally the house itself was sold. A professional auctioneer from the local town was coming to conduct the sale, and whether it was the developer who bought the estate, or the town council who rushed in last minute to save it—in the unlikely event that Lizzie's pleading letter had arrived before the council went into recess for Christmas—this would be the last time she looked out over this view.

She had intended to stay awake all night so she wouldn't miss a minute of her last night at Rottingdean House, but in the end exhaustion drove her to bed, and she was woken by the sound of an engine—several engines—

The horseboxes! Lizzie remembered, jumping out of bed. They had come to take the horses away. Running to the window, she threw back the curtains and peered out. Several big vehicles were already lined up in the yard. She would have to put the bravest face of all on today. Brave and practical, Lizzie concluded, her thoughts racing. There was work to do. The sale and the scandal of a second bankruptcy wouldn't just bring serious buyers in droves to Rottingdean, it would bring rubberneckers from all over the county who would trample the good pastureland to mud, unless she did something about it.

She showered and dressed quickly before running downstairs to the yard. But what she saw confused her. Horses arriving? That couldn't be right.

'You'll have to take them back,' she told the lead driver when he came round to help the grooms to lead the ponies out of their confinement. 'They can't stay here. Everything is being sold today.'

'Sorry, miss, we've got our orders. The horses are being delivered, not taken away,' he informed her as he gestured to his men, who had briefly halted at Lizzie's arrival, to get on with the job.

'But who sent them?'

The man shrugged. 'The new owner? I really don't know. I just have my orders. Six ponies in my care, and another sixteen in the other vehicles.'

'Twenty-two ponies?' Lizzie exclaimed with alarm. 'And how can there be a new owner when the sale hasn't even begun?' She didn't know whether to be glad that a developer would hardly deliver so many horses to a property he intended to demolish, or concerned that the new owner hadn't even troubled to look the place over before dispatching what were clearly valuable animals.

'As I said, I'm afraid I can't give you any more details than I already have, because I don't know anything more,' the man told her, turning away. 'These are the stables?" he asked over his shoulder.

'Yes. And the home paddock is empty, if you want to use it,' she said, pointing away from the house.

Was Chico the new owner? Her heart began to race. He had been locked away with his lawyers. Snatches of conversation they'd had earlier came back to her. *'...the estate is in danger of being lost, and I'd like to help so you can keep it in the family. As your grandmother helped me.'* But she had refused Chico's offer of help, suspecting too many conditions would be attached. Had he just ignored her wishes and gone ahead without telling her?

There was no point being angry that he hadn't confided in her. Power was money, and, while Chico had plenty, she had none. But she wasn't going to lie down and give up. Rottingdean would be left in the best state she could manage—and she had an idea how to raise some more money to share amongst the tenants.

There wasn't much time. The gates were due to open in a few hours in preparation for the sale at midday. She would rally the ground staff, and, with their help, set aside land for paid parking. Hamish could gather his ghillies together and take people on tours of the estate with a view to perhaps adding guided nature trails to the list of attractions at some later date, while Annie could brew tea and start baking.

The Rottingdean café was born, Lizzie thought, feeling upbeat now. Her grandmother's conservator could give tours of the house, while Lizzie could take children to see the animals and new ponies. Raising sufficient funds in a day to support everyone until they could find new jobs was a bit of a pipe dream, but anything was better than nothing, and she wanted to prove that Rottingdean did have a future, and shouldn't be torn down. The Rottingdean Experience was about to be launched on an unsuspecting world.

The Rottingdean Experience was an even bigger success than Lizzie had envisaged. Money poured in. And though these were only small amounts compared to the debt owed, the buckets full of coins and small-value notes represented the pride of the estate to her. The hall where the auction was to be held was full to capacity, and it seemed that everything was going smoothly, until the auctioneer called to say he was indisposed, and there was no one else available to take the sale.

Lizzie faltered—but only for a few seconds. There was someone who could take the sale, she determined.

She dressed up and put on her high-heeled shoes. An auctioneer had to show a bold face to the world, and not seem defeated, and she was nowhere near finished yet.

'Who knows these items better than I do?' she asked the group of representatives from the various institutions with an interest in the outcome of the sale. 'And devils can't be choosers,' she pointed out.

And so it was agreed. Lizzie would take the auction.

'My lords, ladies, and gentlemen,' she began in a firm, upbeat voice, standing on the rostrum where everyone could see her. 'Today we are holding a very unusual and special sale where many of these items have been in the Fane family for centuries, so I hope you all have your funds in place, because I know you're all going to want to spend lots of money.'

A ripple of good-humoured laughter opened the proceedings, and from there the sale flew along at a rate of knots.

* * *

He remained in the background as Lizzie took the sale. He had his people planted in the crowd. Several more were online, and there were a couple on the telephone. He had this sale wrapped up. The bright light that had first attracted him to Lizzie when she was little more than a child was blazing strongly today. Far from being beaten by circumstance, she had this crowd eating out of her hand. As he looked around he noticed that the faces of the staff at Rottingdean had the same zeal as Lizzie's written all over them, yet they were watching her part with what had to be a lifetime of memories for them. They all had true Scottish grit. Nothing was going to get them down. With their life in ruins they had come into their own, because of one petite figure wielding her will as well as her gavel, a tiny woman who was a giant when it came to courage and vision, and getting things done.

A thunderbolt struck him, or maybe it had struck on the day Lizzie walked back into his life. She was the only woman he wanted, and he would do anything it took to persuade her to come back with him to Brazil. But would she ever leave Rottingdean? Would she even trust him enough to let him try to win her back?

Trust had been an issue for both of them, he reflected as he watched Lizzie run the sale with precision and calm assurance, but he had to hope that lack of trust was behind her now, as it was behind him. There were some prizes worth fighting for, and he could be as determined as Lizzie when it came to achieving his goal.

Lizzie drew a deep breath. 'And now the final lot.' She paused for effect and, more than that, to calm herself. She couldn't afford to let her voice shake now. 'Rottingdean

House, ladies and gentlemen. This beautiful home you're standing in now—'

There was an uncomfortable silence, and then one of the representatives from the bank came to the foot of the rostrum to whisper something.

Lizzie felt cheated. She felt as if the auction would have given her time to mourn the loss of her childhood home, and now there was no time.

'My apologies, ladies and gentlemen—I have just learned that a sale has been agreed prior to this auction, so, for today, this auction is over.'

That was it? Lizzie thought, feeling unsteady as she climbed down from the rostrum. How quickly the sale had gone. A lifetime sold off in a matter of minutes—several lifetimes, she reflected, thinking of the ancestors who had lived at Rottingdean before her. How she got down those few rickety wooden steps, she would never know. She was reminded of the first time she'd been put on a pony and had looked for railings to hang onto, only to find there were none. As in life, she reflected wryly. She was on her own now, and had to plan accordingly.

'Excuse me, Miss Lizzie.'

'Yes?' She smiled at the representative from the bank. She bore him no grudges. What was the point when he was only doing his job?

'Should I call you Lady Elizabeth?' he said, blushing bright red.

'Definitely not,' she reassured him. 'Lizzie's fine.' She didn't want anyone calling her Lady Elizabeth Fane when she hadn't earned the title. It was just an accident of birth. And there was something else, Lizzie thought as her mouth quirked with amusement. Maybe she was delirious with sadness, and weary with disappointment, but all she could think about was being in bed with Chico—so she might be wearing high-heeled shoes, but she could state categorically that she was no lady.

'Can I help you with anything?' she said pleasantly, seeing the man from the bank was still hovering.

'The new owner would like to see you,' he explained.

'The new owner?' She looked around. It couldn't be Chico, Lizzie reasoned, because Chico would have made himself known. She hadn't heard from him for three days now. When she spoke to his PA she presumed Chico was back in Brazil. It was the student graduation in a few days, and he would never miss that.

'He's in your grandmother's study.'

'Oh, is he?' Lizzie felt her temper rising, and knew that had more to do with Chico than any slight inflicted by this new owner. 'He couldn't wait to get his feet under the table, I suppose.' She left the man from the bank staring after her anxiously.

She knew the moment she reached the door what she would find behind it.

'Chico,' she said as she walked in. She tried to maintain a calm demeanour, but after being in a room full of sun-starved individuals, dressed in muted heather tones, seeing Chico in all his piratical splendour was quite a shock. He was dressed all in black: black shirt, black jacket, black trousers, with his wild black hair barely tamed for the occasion. He looked as if he had just stepped from the centrefold of a polo magazine. He was quite simply the most bronzed, bold, and beautiful man she had ever seen. Right now, his only flaw, as far as she could tell, was the expression on his face, which was knowing and even faintly amused. He looked every bit the conquering hero. He towered over her, all-powerful, and completely in command, but she refused to be intimidated. At least he'd had the good grace not to sit behind her grandmother's desk, but had chosen to stand by the window overlooking the lake, from where he was regarding her now.

'Lizzie…'

'So, you're the new owner.'

She felt a chill come over her as Chico inclined his head, and remembered her father's words: *Revenge is a dish best served cold.* A sudden spear of dread pierced her as the doubts set in. Was that what this was all about? Was Chico revenging himself for her parents' crimes? He had certainly controlled the sale, she realised now, just as Chico controlled everything else in his life. He did that with his iron will and his bottomless pit of money, so, whatever she had tried to do, the outcome for Rottingdean House was always going to be the same.

'Revenge is a cruel taskmaster, Chico,' she murmured as they locked eyes.

'Revenge,' he murmured thoughtfully. 'I really hadn't seen it that way, Lizzie.' There was something in his eyes that called her doubts foolish. 'I see coming back here as a long-awaited dream.' There was a long silence, and then he added, 'I can still remember the thrill of being invited to the big house. I was quite happy bedding down in the stables while the Brazilian polo team was given comfortable rooms in the house—I was always happiest with the horses, and a bit awkward in company.'

'I remember,' Lizzie murmured, drawn back to that time.

'I should have stayed in the stables. I was safe there, had I but known it at the time.'

'Go on,' she urged softly, sensing Chico had an important memory to share when he fell silent.

'Eduardo had planned to go into town with your grandmother to get her view on a classic car that he was thinking of buying and shipping back to Brazil, and he was going to

take your grandmother to dinner afterwards, to thank her
for her time, while I remained with the grooms. Imagine
my astonishment when I received an invitation via your
mother's personal maid to attend a soirée with Lord and
Lady Fane. I had no idea what a soirée was, and imagined
it was some sort of tea party. I just hoped I wouldn't have
to eat a formal dinner, because Eduardo was still teaching me which cutlery to use.' He paused. 'It all sounds so
silly now, doesn't it?'

'Not to me,' Lizzie argued.

'It was a party of sorts,' he said dryly. 'I was lucky to
get out with my life.'

'I can imagine,' Lizzie agreed as they both thought back.

'I was so young—such a fool. I had no idea that at this
type of party dress was optional, or that drink and drugs
were mandatory, along with a host of pretty young boys
and girls just over the age of consent. I didn't realise that
money was changing hands either, or that I was supposed
to be the star turn. I didn't realise how strait-laced I was
until I walked into that room and witnessed the "performance", as Serena described it, which was well under way
by the time I arrived—youth-on-youth, girl-on-girl, and
every other variation on a theme—all free to view in a
tangle of naked limbs on a bed decked out with black satin
sheets, to a soundtrack of moans and hard metal.'

'You and me next,' Serena had purred in his ear as she
tottered about in her ridiculously high heels and marabou-
trimmed negligee. With one hand she had reached for a
drink from the tray the naked butler was holding, while
she used her other hand to attempt to grope Chico through
his pants. 'I've been saving myself for you,' she had informed him seductively.

'What did you say to my mother?' Lizzie asked, jolting
him out of these thoughts.

'I think not,' he explained, which made Lizzie laugh.

'And then you backed your way out of the door as quickly as you could?'

'You guessed,' he said, omitting to tell Lizzie that her mother's expression had hardened as she'd regarded him coldly.

'This isn't a free choice, Chico,' Serena had informed him. 'You're a groom here at Rottingdean, and as such you're a servant who will do as you are told.'

'I'm afraid not, my lady,' he'd replied. Being innocent of such things back then, he had no doubt that his eyes had been wide as saucers.

'You will be afraid if you don't do exactly as I say,' Serena had promised. 'You've seen too much, so if you leave now I'll say you raped me—and I have at least twenty witnesses to back me up.'

At that point he'd noticed Lord Fane for the first time. The grand aristocrat had been seated in a chair that looked something like a throne, with a naked girl kneeling at his feet. As their eyes had met across a scene more reminiscent of Sodom and Gomorrah than the respectable stately home Chico had thought he was staying in, the expression in Lizzie's father's eyes had assured him that what Serena said Serena would make good on, and that Lizzie's father would have no hesitation in backing her mother up.

She suspected there might be more Chico could tell her, but was holding back, because it would damn her parents, rather than Chico, and the last thing Chico wanted was to hurt her. The idea of her mother hitting on Chico when he had expected so much more of the aristocracy sickened her. She was determined to get right to the bottom of it now. 'Is there anything else?' she asked him bluntly. 'Anything you're not telling me. You might as well get it all out now.

Remember what I told you—I'm not that same girl now, and we trust each other, don't we?'

'What do you want me to tell you? I was naïve.'

'And I was fifteen,' she countered.

'I had no excuse,' Chico insisted, still determined to beat himself up. 'I grew up in the *barrio*—I saw my brother killed in front of me—I had a father in jail and a mother on the game, and still I came here to the Highlands, and allowed myself to be seduced by the beauty of the countryside, and the kindness of the people, and I failed entirely to see the same rot in this grand old house that had existed in my tin shack.'

'Only because you expected so much more of us,' Lizzie argued, 'and in the end we're just people. It doesn't matter where we come from. We're all human beings—some flawed, some not. I'm only sorry that, having escaped the gutter, you found yourself here, mired in another type of filth. I've been surrounded by lies all my life, Chico. Tell me we're not going to lie to each other now.'

'You're right,' he agreed, 'except for one thing. I don't regret coming here with Eduardo. If I hadn't come here, we wouldn't have met.' His lips curved in a smile and then, seeing her expression, he turned serious again. 'Are you still worried about me buying the estate?'

Lizzie thought for a moment, and then said honestly, 'I can't deny it will take some getting used to—and I'm not sure where it's going to leave the people who work here, and that's what concerns me.'

'It will leave them exactly where they've always been. This will be my tribute to a very special lady—your grandmother. I think she would be very pleased to know that more children from the slums will be coming here as I did.'

'So that's your plan?' Lizzie exclaimed.

'What did you think?'

'I don't know what I thought,' she admitted, shaking her head. 'But this is such a surprise—a wonderful surprise.'

'I've bought the house and everything in it, so you can work with me. Or you can stand in my way, if you prefer, though I wouldn't advise it,' Chico said wryly. 'When I'm set on a plan, I always carry it through.'

He wanted them to work together? It was an extraordinary, far-sighted plan, but what could she offer the children? She didn't have a diploma, let alone a peg to hang her hat. Were the children supposed to wait until she resolved those issues?

'Could I live here?'

'I would hope so,' Chico confirmed. 'Where are you going now?' he demanded, coming to stand in her way.

'I have to think about this. I need to get back on my feet again first.'

'Yes,' he agreed. 'You do. And?'

'That means ploughing my own furrow, not walking in yours.'

'But you're a crucial part of my plan, Lizzie. I won't let you go so easily this time.'

'You can't stop me,' she said in her most reasonable tone.

Chico's black eyes changed. She knew that look. 'Don't you dare,' she warned him. 'If you kiss me, I'll—'

'You'll what?' Grabbing her close, he cupped her chin and made her look at him.

Lizzie felt so good in his arms, he had to close his eyes for a moment so he could absorb just how good. She was like every Christmas gift come at once—better even than he remembered.

'You barbarian,' she flashed when he pulled back. 'How dare you come in here and kiss me?'

'How dare I? Really?' His lips tugged with amusement,

which only made her madder than before. Her eyes turned black, her lips were swollen, and her nipples thrust imperatively against the fine lace of her bra. 'I might ride to your rescue occasionally, but I'm no saint.'

Before she had a chance to argue with him, he drove his mouth down on hers, claiming the last thing that interested him at Rottingdean. And then, with a fierce sound of hunger and need, she laced her fingers through his hair to keep him close.

CHAPTER FIFTEEN

HE HAD NEVER experienced such a rush of desire before. This was a kiss like no other; an embrace he doubted either of them would ever forget. It was as if all the forces of nature had come together to bind them close. They could argue all they liked, but the fates would not allow them to defy their destiny. When he finally released her, Lizzie's face was flushed to show that the blood was pumping fiercely through her veins. But it wasn't just lust driving her.

'You can't have everything at Rottingdean, Chico,' she told him. 'You can't buy me along with the Chippendale chairs.'

'I don't want to buy you,' he fired back. 'I don't see you as one of the fixtures and fittings,' and just as she was about to get started, he added, 'but I don't see why I can't have you.' And catching her close, he smiled down. 'Why fight what we both want, Lizzie?'

'I might want it,' she argued angrily, 'but I've got more sense.'

'More sense than to do what?' he challenged.

'To love you,' she blurted out, surprising him with her ferocity. 'I've got more sense than to love you.' With an angry huff, she turned her face away. 'And now I'm going to check on the horses,' she said gruffly, 'and when I've done that, I'll pack a bag and you'll never have to see me again—'

'Not so fast.' He caught her close. 'You're not going to leave here, and desert everyone before you've even heard my plan?'

'I no longer have a place here,' she said proudly. 'Rottingdean doesn't belong to the Fane family. It belongs to you. The estate is no longer my responsibility.'

'So, will you say goodbye to the staff on your way out?' he demanded mildly.

She made an angry, impatient sound in reply.

'Would you mind moving away from the door, please?'

'Yes, I'd mind,' he assured her, standing firm. 'Don't tar me with the same brush as your parents, Lizzie. I'm not here to take anything. I'm here to give. I want to restore the estate so that everyone has the chance of a good future. I understand the uncertainty you've all been through, and I want to bring it to an end. I know you're angry now, because this change of ownership has happened so fast, but don't act on impulse. Stay and we can work miracles here.'

'You can't just make everything right,' she said. 'You can't just walk back into Rottingdean House and expect to pick up where we left off.'

'Why not? Why not, Lizzie?' he demanded fiercely. 'We can do anything we want to, if we want it enough.'

She drew breath for a moment, and then slowly relaxed. 'Do you remember this?' she said, pushing back her sleeve.

'That's not the friendship bracelet I made for you?' He shook his head with surprise. 'You've still got it after all these years?' He saw the hurt in her eyes, and understood how Lizzie had felt when she thought he had deserted her. 'If there'd been any other way…'

There was a long silence and then she said softly, 'I feel like you, in that I'm glad you came to Scotland, because you and Eduardo inspired me. I would never have been ready for you to leave.'

'And I didn't want to leave,' he admitted. 'I raged against it.'

'My mother would have destroyed you. I know that now. No one turns down Serena, but you did. That was your only sin. My father's a violent alcoholic, who would have ruined what little remained of the estate so my grandmother had good reason to take the power to do that out of his hands. I remember my mother swearing at my grandmother on that last day, saying she didn't care if they were thrown out, because there were richer pickings for a woman like my mother who still had her looks. There was a lot of gossip after they left, and even if I didn't understand half of it at the time, I know my grandmother wouldn't have been granted custody of me, if it hadn't been bad. And why would Grannie allow me to come on your course in Brazil, if she didn't believe in your innocence? I think she was pleased I won your scholarship, because she wanted justice to prevail, and giving me her blessing was her way of apologising to you for the harm done to you by my parents.'

'And what did you think, Lizzie?'

'Apart from the hurt when you left?' She shrugged. 'I just feel awful about the whole episode now. I should have spoken out. I should have confronted my parents in front of witnesses and called them liars to their faces.'

'No one wants to believe badly of their parents, Lizzie. We make excuses for them, and always try to find some redeeming feature.'

'That's our common bond,' she said with a small smile. 'That, and learning to trust again.'

'You've been talking to Maria.'

'Yes, I have,' she admitted, 'and she filled in even more of the blanks than you have done.'

'Running wild in the *barrio*?' he suggested, slanting a wry smile.

Lizzie laughed as she admitted, 'Something like that.'

'And your grandmother. What did she tell you?'

'She would never say a word against her son, or my mother. Old-fashioned values prevailed, I suppose—family pride, and all that. Preserving what little remained of our reputation took up most of her time, and the rest she devoted to repairing what my father had destroyed.'

'Your parents won't have the chance to destroy anything more now I'm here.'

'Agreed. I doubt they'd take you on.' Shaking her head, Lizzie laughed.

'I suppose there are some compensations to my being the barbarian they talk about in the press.'

Lizzie angled her chin to stare up at him. 'A barbarian with a great way with horses, and that's what matters. So, where will you start?'

'My immediate plans?' Chico's eyes had begun to burn with humour.

'No,' she warned without much force as he ran one fingertip lightly down her cheek. 'Not those.'

'I'm going to expand the training and breeding programme at Rottingdean,' he said, pulling away. 'But first I'm going back to Brazil and you're coming with me.'

When she began to protest that she had duties here in Scotland to attend to, he added, 'Before you say no, consider this: you need that diploma on your wall, Lizzie, if you have any thoughts at all of involving yourself in the business here.'

'Working under you?'

'If that's your preference.'

Chico's eyes were the most eloquent eyes she'd ever

seen, and right now they were inviting her to do more than help him with his equine breeding programme.

Was she in danger of taking herself too seriously? Lizzie wondered as she gave Chico a stern look. Yes. Quite suddenly, sleeping with the boss seemed like a hard-earned perk that she was most definitely entitled to, rather than a reckless risk that could land her in trouble.

'Yes,' she said, holding Chico's wicked gaze with a challenging stare. 'I think I might take you up on that offer. And working under you would be my preference too—at least, to begin with.'

Chico kicked the door shut behind him, and she was in his arms before it slammed shut. 'I've missed you,' he husked, and that was all he had time for before she was reaching for his clothes and ripping them off.

Sweeping the papers off the desk, he pressed her back. 'Let's not waste time,' he said, staring deep into her eyes.

'Who's wasting time?' she demanded, having already unbuckled his belt. 'I take my barbarians as I find them—preferably naked, but when it's an emergency, I'll take whatever I can get.'

'I trust you expect me to behave like a barbarian, rather than to waste too much time on unnecessary preparations?'

'You got that right.' She groaned as he took her deep.

She had never been more aroused. Chico was big and tough and hungry, and she liked nothing better than to feed his appetite. She loved it when he was tender and gentle with her, but she liked him fierce best of all. 'Just don't stop,' she instructed as he thrust deep. 'At least not until I tell you to.'

'Understood. So, to summarise—'

'Forget the summary and get on with it. I'm close.'

'You're the best asset I've got,' he said, setting up a deliciously rhythmical pattern of deep, firm thrusts, 'so you'll come back to Brazil with me—'

'I'll come anywhere,' she assured him, hanging on by the slimmest of threads.

'You'll graduate and play in the match, and then we'll discuss the details of your duties—'

'Stop—' Clinging to him, she drew a breath. 'Nothing's been decided yet.'

'It has by me,' Chico informed her coolly as she hung suspended in his erotic net.

'Then it's no deal,' she said.

'Would you like me to stop?'

'I'd like you to finish what you started.'

'That can be arranged...at a price.'

'Which is?'

'I need you to work with me. The team I'm going to put in place will need your input.'

'I need your input.'

Chico's teeth flashed white against his dark skin as he laughed down at her. 'I have to say this is the first time I've discussed contract terms under these conditions.'

'I should hope so. Now, could you just—?'

She cried out as Chico did exactly what she needed him to do—and did it thoroughly and very well indeed.

'That was amazing,' she panted. 'You really are the best.'

'Out of how many?'

So few she wouldn't even embarrass herself by mentioning the number, and not one of them could make her scream. 'Stop looking for compliments,' she said as Chico raked his hair, making wild even wilder. 'You know you're the best.'

'Money's no object, Lizzie. You can buy all the stock and equipment that you need—'

'Are we going to just talk about business?' she interrupted. 'Because, if we are—'

'I'm placing all my business with you,' Chico assured her as his mouth curved in a wicked smile.

Lizzie pretended to think about this for a moment. 'Can we move this to the sofa? Only, I've got some business I want to discuss with you, and this desk is hard.'

'Whatever you say.'

Chico lifted her into his arms without breaking that most critical of connections between them.

'This is the benefit of making love with a very strong man, I suppose,' she commented as he lowered her carefully down onto the cushions without compromising her pleasure in any way.

'I'm not letting you go,' he confirmed, starting to move again. 'In fact you're not going anywhere for quite some time. I take it you're in agreement with that?'

'Fully,' she said, groaning as he upped the pace.

Still not entirely sure how they'd make it work once they left this room, she only knew that right now they were as close as two people could be, and something told her that this time when Chico left, they'd leave together.

They arrived back in Brazil to a fiesta. It was hard to be anything but excited when the sound of that hot South American beat thrummed through her body like an invitation to sin.

'Okay?' Chico said, turning to her.

If only she could stop wanting him for a few minutes. It had been bad enough on the plane when she had thought the flight would never end, but now her body was demanding Chico's most urgent attention. He had piloted the plane from Buenos Aires in black jeans and a black casual shirt with the sleeves rolled back, looking like the man she could quite happily spend the rest of her life in bed with.

'I asked you, are you okay?' he pointed out.

'Most definitely,' she said, wondering how long it would be before Chico took her into his arms and kissed her hard.

'Preparations for the graduation ceremony are well under way,' he said, bursting her bubble.

Yes, she was a student—Chico's student—and she had to behave as such, which meant no fraternisation, and absolutely no sex. At least, not all the time.

Danny was waiting by the Jeep, ready to take them to the ranch. They exchanged a warm hug. 'Welcome home,' Danny exclaimed, holding Lizzie at arm's length so she could assess her friend. 'Are you okay?'

'Of course I am.'

'Yes, I can see that,' Danny commented wryly.

'How are you?'

'I've been worried about you,' Danny admitted, 'with everything going on back in Scotland.'

'It was a great send-off. I'm only sorry you couldn't be there.'

'I'm sure you said goodbye for me too.'

'I did, and I thought about the times when the three of us—you, me, and Grannie, were together and really happy.'

'I'll drive,' Chico stated flatly, holding out his hand for the keys.

The two girls exchanged a glance, and were forced to wait until Chico had dropped them off outside the grooms' accommodation before they could discuss him.

'So you haven't got him fully trained yet,' Danny observed dryly.

Lizzie hummed. 'Don't worry. I'm working on it.'

As they carried her case upstairs, Lizzie began to tell

Danny more about the trip back to Scotland—the ugly and the good.

'You know what your trouble is?' Danny remarked as they flopped down on the bed. 'You and Chico are so stubborn—you both want to be in control.'

'There is no me and Chico,' Lizzie insisted.

'Of course there is,' Danny argued. 'You just can't see it yet—mainly because you're waiting for something to happen, when you should be out there making it happen. This isn't like you, Lizzie. Go get your man. Wrestle him to the ground and claim your prize.'

'I'm sure Chico would be thrilled.'

'I'm sure he would too. And I'm not being sarcastic. You owe it to Chico.'

'I owe him what?'

'What's the betting that he's waiting for you right now?' Danny demanded. 'He'll be heartbroken if you don't do this one small thing for him.'

'What? Wrestle him to the ground?' Lizzie laughed. 'Much as that image tempts me—'

'If you both go on being too proud to admit how you feel about each other, then you're letting a good thing go to waste. And that's all I have to say on the matter.' Leaping off the bed, Danny turned to look at her. 'Are you still here?'

'Not for long,' Lizzie confirmed, pushing her way through the door.

CHAPTER SIXTEEN

THERE WAS NO reply when Lizzie knocked on the front door of the ranch house. Thinking better of her mission, she turned to go—then stopped. She tried the handle. The door was unlocked. Fate, huh?

Walking in, she called out, 'Hello…'

The big house echoed back at her. Perhaps Chico was taking a shower…

Well, she knew where his bedroom was. Guessing everyone else was out of the house, helping to prepare for the graduation ceremony, she ran up the stairs and paused on the landing. She could hear water running. Now she was tiptoeing as if she was an intruder. She was an intruder. She was here without invitation. Chico would probably remind her that she was a student here, and throw her out…

The bedroom door was slightly ajar, the shower door too. She slipped inside the room, and stood watching. Lizzie the voyeur? She couldn't help herself. Chico had his back to her so she could indulge herself all she liked, and she loved his back view, especially with water cascading over his muscles. With his head thrown back as he stood beneath the powerful stream of water, Chico was a glorious, and a tempting sight.

This was insane, Lizzie concluded as she kicked off her shoes. Someone should snap their fingers and wake her up.

What exactly did she have to lose?

She made it halfway across the room when Chico stilled. She should have remembered how keenly tuned his senses were. She stopped dead as he opened the shower door and walked out. Dripping water, he proved conclusively that his front view was even better than the back.

'Lizzie Fane,' he said, gripping her shoulders. 'You pick the strangest times to call a meeting.'

'Who said anything about a meeting?'

'I can't think why else you'd be here.'

'Can't you?' She held his gaze. Chico's long black eyelashes were spiked and wet, and his eyes were laughing down at her. Water was dripping from his wild, thick hair, and he looked—there were no words, and for a few crucial seconds she was speechless, motionless, and asking to be kissed.

'I hope you like cold showers.'

She shrieked as he lifted her over his shoulder.

Water was pounding like Niagara in the shower, and he was right: it was freezing.

'So,' he said, holding her in front of him. 'What do you have to say to me?'

Chico kept on laughing as she gasped for breath, and the next thing she knew, he was kissing her. Not just kissing her—he slammed her against the wall of the shower and devoured her. 'I've missed you, Lizzie,' he husked, his stubble rough against her neck.

'I want you,' she gasped out.

Chico was already working on her clothes, and they were both laughing now, because it was proving almost impossible to take them off. They were welded to her body by the water, and she had to help him, wriggling and swearing under her breath, until finally she was down to her bra and pants. 'This last bit should be easy,' she declared.

'So, let me.' Chico smiled as he slowly peeled off the last of her clothing with a frustrating lack of speed. Then, holding her face between his big, rough hands, he stared into her eyes and he kissed her. 'I love you, Lizzie Fane,' he whispered against her mouth. 'I've always loved you.'

'But—'

'No buts,' Chico cautioned, placing his forefinger over her lips. 'We'll work it out.'

She stared into his eyes and believed him. This was the man she'd waited for, and nothing would ever part them again. Chico loved her. What more did she need to know?

Chico's kiss was so tender, so deep, so cherishing, but when they pulled apart and she saw the smallest adjustment in his gaze she read the invitation, and in an instant tender turned fierce.

'I need you too,' Chico assured her, and, dipping at the knees, he proved just how much.

Breath left her lungs in a rush. She'd forgotten how wild her hunger for him could be. She'd also forgotten how powerful and effective Chico could be. He was an amazing lover. Pinning her hands above her head, he supported her against the wall with one arm as he thrust into her, until the collision of hot and cold, and mind-blowing sensation became too much to bear and tipped her over the edge. She broke into laughter as he soothed her down. 'That was so good you have to do it again just so I can be sure I'm not dreaming.'

'That was no dream,' he assured her as he switched off the shower.

'But we'd better be sure,' she said.

'Okay, but not here,' he agreed. 'You're clean enough for now.'

She still had her legs locked around his waist as Chico grabbed a couple of towels and walked her into the bedroom. He was still hard and deep inside her, and still obviously hungry, and so was she. It was a long time later when he dried her hair, and wrapped her in one of his big, soft towels. 'You can sleep now,' he said, dropping kisses on her brow.

'I hope you're joking,' she whispered, reaching for him.

'Just testing,' he murmured.

'Then, get under the covers and test me some more.'

He laughed against her mouth as he stretched out his long, powerful limbs on the bed. 'I think I might just do that.'

'Don't think about it,' she urged. 'Just act on instinct.'

'If you say so,' Chico murmured dryly.

Their mouths were almost touching, and before he did as she asked he kissed her in the way she loved to be kissed. She would never tire of Chico kissing her, just as she would never tire of stroking him, or mapping his powerful muscles and the wide spread of his shoulders. He was so bronzed, so hard, so big, so perfect. Turning her, he found her with his hand, and as she arched her back to make it easy for him he entered her again, making his strokes deep and regular, and slow, so they could both savour each lazy thrust. She exclaimed shakily as his hand worked skilfully to the same easy rhythm.

'Don't hold back,' he growled against her neck. 'We've got all night, so why not indulge yourself?'

She didn't need any more encouragement, and let go, her muscles convulsing around him as she gratefully and powerfully lost control.

When she woke dawn was streaming in through the windows. She was in Chico's arms, and he was watching her. She had no idea how many times they'd made love, only that each time had been better than the last.

'Well?' he murmured. 'Are you ready for the new day?'

He was doing something incredible—and not just with his hands—so all she could manage was a sleepy moan of agreement.

'Brazen hussy,' he murmured, pressing his hand into the small of her back to make her even more available to him.

'Barbarian,' she countered as Chico took her buttocks in a firm grip and began to move.

And now one of his big hands had moved to tease her nipples, while the other worked rhythmically on the heat at her core. She was a slave to sensation, and Chico was the master of seduction. It wouldn't have mattered if she'd been wearing armour rather than lying naked in his bed, nothing on earth could have stopped the wave of sensation that roared up inside her and spilled out in screams.

'What's this?' he murmured later when she was quiet. He'd caught one fat tear on his fingertip and was staring at it in surprise.

She would have to go home after the graduation. She would have to leave him.

'We will never be parted again, Lizzie Fane,' Chico told her as if he could read her mind. 'We've spent too long apart already.'

'But—'

'I told you, no buts. We're going to do this thing together, you and me. We're going to rebuild the Rottingdean estate and make it the go-to place for polo training and polo ponies in Europe, and we're going to change the lives of hordes of children, while we keep this place right up there too.'

'But how are we going to do that, when Scotland and Brazil are half a world apart?'

Chico smiled. 'The world's a small place when we have private jets, and teams with people like Maria and Annie in them, and we have the Internet at our command. Believe me, it can be managed, Lizzie.'

'Managed between us,' she confirmed. 'Just thought I should check,' she added, smiling, when Chico shot her a look.

'We'll make a great team, too,' he confirmed. 'Though you still have a lot to learn,' he added after a moment's thought.

'Like you have a lot to learn about Rottingdean?'

Chico's answer was to roll her on the bed. 'I'm going to start as I mean to go on. You can give me a full rundown on the estate as we continue our activities.'

'On the contrary, Senhor Fernandez,' she said, wriggling free. 'I would hate you to think you must carry the burden of leadership alone.'

'Am I arguing?' Chico said, his mouth curving in a contented smile as Lizzie mounted him and pinned him to the bed.

EPILOGUE

THERE WERE NO windswept plains peopled by wild men and magnificent horses as Chico and Lizzie had temporarily swapped their home in Brazil for their home in Scotland for this, the most important day of their lives.

The weather was being kind to them in the leafy glen where Rottingdean House sat like a symbol of longevity, surrounded by snow-capped mountains under a sky of silver-blue. Lush green grass, purple heather and rich black peat took the place of swaying pampas grass, and, instead of mountain lions and wolves, a noble stag with ten-point antlers stood guard over the glassy loch. The only sound to break the silence was the eagle's stirring cry as it soared from its eyrie on the first hunt of the day, but now the skirl of the pipes set the scene as the entire village turned out to toast the newly-weds, as they walked back in a winding procession to the big house from the small kirk in the village where Chico and Lizzie had exchanged their marriage vows.

In spite of protesting that she was allergic to weddings, and that she would prefer to remain in the background throughout, when they arrived back at the house it was Danny who caught the bride's bouquet. Lizzie had made sure of it. 'Though you can't leave me yet,' Lizzie insisted.

'Not now you're my right-hand man, so to speak. I'm going to need you around.'

'Feed me enough chocolate and I'll see what I can do,' Danny promised, her cheeks flushing red as Tiago came towards her. 'The one thing I don't want,' she added to Lizzie in a heated whisper, 'is a wild polo man.'

'They're not so bad,' Lizzie reassured her with a glance at Chico, who was doing the rounds of people she'd known all her life, and with whom he was already on the easiest of terms. Chico got on with everyone, she reflected happily.

'Give me a pipe and slippers man any day of the week.' Danny sniffed. 'And now, if you will excuse me, I have some mild-mannered folk to catch up with.'

'You'll be back,' Lizzie predicted with a smile, noticing how Tiago was watching her friend as Danny slipped away into the crowd.

It was a thrill for Lizzie to see that, instead of uncertainty, there was cause for celebration at Rottingdean. And to see Maria being brought into the fold by Annie and all the other women in the village made her confident that the two worlds could be combined.

The log fire was blazing in the hall, and people were flowing back and forth through the newly renovated rooms. There was still a lot to do, and they would have to close the house for a while to complete the improvements, but for now there were colourful, seasonal decorations—berries, twigs, and flowers—and that most important diploma hanging over the door of Lizzie's office. Her grandmother would be pleased, Lizzie thought, because the estate was safe for the next generation, and the next. In fact, the next generation was growing happily and well, according to the doctor she had visited with Chico to confirm her pregnancy. Stroking her stomach, she wondered how long it would be before this next generation sat in a basket saddle on the back of their mildest Shetland pony.

It had all turned out well in the end, she reflected. Even the end-of-term match had gone well. They'd won.

'Of course they won,' was all Chico had said. 'What do you think I've trained you to do? To lose?'

As if she didn't know—anything less than a win was unthinkable for him. But she'd forgive him. For every arrogant comment and autocratic stare, Chico's personality was balanced with kindness and care.

'There will be reels and dancing,' she warned him when he came up to her side.

'So long as we don't have to stay too long,' he growled, dropping kisses on her neck as he held her lightly.

'Don't you ever think of anything else?'

'Do you?'

'Must you ask me such difficult questions on our wedding day?'

'Only one more,' Chico promised, smiling wickedly.

'Which is?' Lizzie demanded as they linked fingers.

'Will you live with me and be my love, for ever, Lizzie Fernandez?'

As their bodies were only a hair's breadth away, and the temptation to bring them a lot closer was overwhelming her in hot, hungry waves, she could only say yes.

'I do agree. We shouldn't stay too long at the party,' she said, reaching for Chico's hands. 'For ever,' she pledged, standing on tiptoe to kiss her wild polo man.

'I'm pleased with your decision,' he said as he lifted Lizzie into his arms.

'Hey—I thought we'd stay a while.'

'Did I say that?' Chico frowned.

Lizzie pulled back to give him a look, but Chico had turned serious.

'We must thank Eduardo and your grandmother for bringing us together,' he declared, heading for the stairs.

'I hope they're looking down on us,' Lizzie agreed softly.

Chico thought about this for a moment. 'For now, that's okay, but when we reach the bedroom?' He shrugged.

'You're such a barbarian,' Lizzie murmured with satisfaction, snuggling close.

'Yes, I am,' Chico agreed. 'Aren't you glad?'

* * * * *

COMING NEXT MONTH FROM

HARLEQUIN *Presents*®

Available March 17, 2015

#3321 VIRGIN'S SWEET REBELLION
The Chatsfield
by Kate Hewitt
Ben Chatsfield knows he should call "Cut!" when the press run a
story that he's involved with Olivia Harrington...but then he learns
his leading lady is completely untouched! Something Ben plans to
rectify before the credits roll on their fake relationship...

#3322 THE BILLIONAIRE'S BRIDAL BARGAIN
Bound by Gold
by Lynne Graham
To get his hands on her Mediterranean island inheritance,
Cesare Sabatino *must* wed innocent Lizzie Whitaker...and ensure
she's carrying his heir! Legendary for his powers of persuasion,
Cesare will show Lizzie the many *pleasurable* benefits of wearing
this tycoon's ring...

#3323 THE ITALIAN'S DEAL FOR I DO
Society Weddings
by Jennifer Hayward
In order to regain control of the fashion empire that's rightfully his,
Rocco Mondelli must prove his playboy days are over. His secret
weapon? Supermodel-in-hiding Olivia Fitzgerald...and the power to
ruin her if she refuses to play his loving fiancée!

#3324 HIS DIAMOND OF CONVENIENCE
by Maisey Yates
Twelve years ago Victoria Calder made a terrible mistake, and
now, finally, she has the chance to atone. And if that means going
toe-to-toe with the arresting Dmitri Markin, she's prepared to step
into the ring...and put his on her finger!

HPCNM0315RA

#3325 CARRYING THE GREEK'S HEIR
One Night With Consequences
by Sharon Kendrick

Since Ellie Brooks met Alekto Sarantos, everything has changed. First she was fired. Now she's pregnant with the ruthless Greek's baby! Ellie demands Alekto legitimize their unborn child, and he shocks them both...by agreeing to her outrageous request!

#3326 AT THE BRAZILIAN'S COMMAND
Hot Brazilian Nights!
by Susan Stephens

Polo champion Tiago Santos needs a wife who understands that this Brazilian stallion *won't* be tamed! Practical Danny Cameron is the perfect candidate. But as their wedding night approaches, the sensual rhythm of the samba leaves Danny wanting more...

#3327 THE SHEIKH'S PRINCESS BRIDE
Desert Vows
by Annie West

With a kingdom to rule, sheikh Tariq of Al-Sharath has no time—or wish—to find a bride, but his children need a mother. Princess Samira of Jazeer could be the answer. But she has one *very* testing condition...no sex!

#3328 OLIVERO'S OUTRAGEOUS PROPOSAL
by Kate Walker

For Dario Olivero, Alyse Gregory was just a way to reap revenge against his estranged half brother. But Alyse carries the key to the family acceptance he's always craved, and realizing just how much trouble she's in, he can't turn away...

YOU CAN FIND MORE INFORMATION ON UPCOMING HARLEQUIN® TITLES, FREE EXCERPTS AND MORE AT WWW.HARLEQUIN.COM.

HPCNM0315RB

REQUEST YOUR FREE BOOKS!

2 FREE NOVELS PLUS
2 FREE GIFTS!

YES! Please send me 2 FREE Harlequin Presents® novels and my 2 FREE gifts (gifts are worth about $10). After receiving them, if I don't wish to receive any more books, I can return the shipping statement marked "cancel." If I don't cancel, I will receive 6 brand-new novels every month and be billed just $4.30 per book in the U.S. or $4.99 per book in Canada. That's a saving of at least 14% off the cover price! It's quite a bargain! Shipping and handling is just 50¢ per book in the U.S. and 75¢ per book in Canada.* I understand that accepting the 2 free books and gifts places me under no obligation to buy anything. I can always return a shipment and cancel at any time. Even if I never buy another book, the two free books and gifts are mine to keep forever.

106/306 HDN FVRK

Name _____ (PLEASE PRINT)

Address _____ Apt. #

City _____ State/Prov. _____ Zip/Postal Code

Signature (if under 18, a parent or guardian must sign)

Mail to the **Harlequin® Reader Service:**
IN U.S.A.: P.O. Box 1867, Buffalo, NY 14240-1867
IN CANADA: P.O. Box 609, Fort Erie, Ontario L2A 5X3

**Are you a current subscriber to Harlequin Presents books
and want to receive the larger-print edition?
Call 1-800-873-8635 or visit www.ReaderService.com.**

* Terms and prices subject to change without notice. Prices do not include applicable taxes. Sales tax applicable in N.Y. Canadian residents will be charged applicable taxes. Offer not valid in Quebec. This offer is limited to one order per household. Not valid for current subscribers to Harlequin Presents books. All orders subject to credit approval. Credit or debit balances in a customer's account(s) may be offset by any other outstanding balance owed by or to the customer. Please allow 4 to 6 weeks for delivery. Offer available while quantities last.

Your Privacy—The Harlequin® Reader Service is committed to protecting your privacy. Our Privacy Policy is available online at www.ReaderService.com or upon request from the Harlequin Reader Service.

We make a portion of our mailing list available to reputable third parties that offer products we believe may interest you. If you prefer that we not exchange your name with third parties, or if you wish to clarify or modify your communication preferences, please visit us at www.ReaderService.com/consumerschoice or write to us at Harlequin Reader Service Preference Service, P.O. Box 9062, Buffalo, NY 14269. Include your complete name and address.

HP13

"I'm willing to offer you a substantial amount of money to go through a marriage ceremony with me."

Her lashes fluttered in shock because he had knocked her for six. Inexplicably, his cool sophistication and smooth delivery made the fantastic proposition he had just offered seem almost workaday and acceptable. "Seriously? *Just* a marriage ceremony? But what would you get out of that?"

Cesare told her about his grandmother's deep attachment to the island Lizzie had inherited and his grandmother's approaching surgery. As she listened, Lizzie nodded slowly, strangely touched by the softer tone he couldn't help employing when talking about the old lady. His screened gaze and the faint hint of flush along his spectacular cheekbones encouraged her scrutiny to linger with helpless curiosity. He was not quite as cold and tough as he seemed on the surface, she acknowledged in surprise.

"For the sake of appearances we would have to pretend that the marriage was the real deal for a few months at least."

"And the 'having a child' bit? Where does that come in?" Lizzie could not resist asking.

"Whether it comes into our arrangement or not is up to you. I will pay generously for the right to take my grandmother to the island for a visit, and if we were to contrive to meet the *full* terms of the will, you and your sister would stand to collect a couple of million pounds, at the very least, from selling Lionos to me," he spelled out quietly. "I am an extremely wealthy man and I will pay a high price to bring the island back into my family."

A convenient marriage soon becomes anything but, when Lizzie and Cesare give in to the passion that burns between them...especially when Lizzie becomes pregnant with his child!

Find out what happens next in
THE BILLIONAIRE'S BRIDAL BARGAIN,
available April 2015 wherever
Harlequin Presents® books and ebooks are sold.

www.Harlequin.com